Olivia heard a

She scooped her s   inside the bathroom within the motel suite.

The mercenaries must have found her. Again.

She blinked back tears, trying to convince herself that Ryker would survive.

That they would all survive.

"Olivia? Are you in there?" Ryker's familiar voice made her knees go weak.

She opened the door, grateful to see Ryker standing there. "What happened? Is everyone all right?"

"Yeah, but we need to hit the road. Now."

She stepped into the suite but stopped abruptly when she saw the two men unmoving on the floor.

"Thankfully, they must not have realized I had Duncan and Mike with me. I'm sure if they'd known, they would have come with more men."

More men. It was horrifying to think that there would be more men coming after them.

Forever, or at least until they'd gotten what they'd wanted.

Laura Scott is a nurse by day and an author by night. She has always loved romance and had read faith-based books by Grace Livingston Hill in her teenage years. She's thrilled to have published over twenty-five books for Love Inspired Suspense. She has two adult children and lives in Milwaukee, Wisconsin, with her husband of over thirty years. Please visit Laura at laurascottbooks.com, as she loves to hear from her readers.

Books by Laura Scott

Love Inspired Suspense

Justice Seekers

Soldier's Christmas Secrets
Guarded by the Soldier

Callahan Confidential

Shielding His Christmas Witness
The Only Witness
Christmas Amnesia
Shattered Lullaby
Primary Suspect
Protecting His Secret Son

True Blue K-9 Unit: Brooklyn

Copycat Killer

Visit the Author Profile page at Harlequin.com for more titles.

GUARDED BY THE SOLDIER

LAURA SCOTT

LOVE INSPIRED SUSPENSE
INSPIRATIONAL ROMANCE

LOVE INSPIRED® SUSPENSE
INSPIRATIONAL ROMANCE

ISBN-13: 978-1-335-72181-5

Guarded by the Soldier

This edition published by arrangement with Harlequin Books S.A.

For questions and comments about the quality of this book, please contact us at CustomerService@Harlequin.com.

Love Inspired
22 Adelaide St. West, 40th Floor
Toronto, Ontario M5H 4E3, Canada
www.Harlequin.com

Printed in U.S.A.

Recycling programs for this product may not exist in your area.

Help us, O God of our salvation,
for the glory of thy name: and deliver us,
and purge away our sins, for thy name's sake.
−Psalm 79:9

This book is dedicated to my niece Taylour Rose Iding, DPT. Welcome to health care. I'm so proud of you!

ONE

Olivia Habush closed and locked the office door, then shouldered her large zebra-striped bag before heading out the back door of the church. The early June evening was warm, and she resisted the urge to fan herself. Early summer in the quaint town of Harrisburg, Illinois, was much warmer than what she was used to when she'd lived in Madison, Wisconsin.

The edges of her oversize blouse flapped around her large pregnant belly as she made her way across the street. Mrs. Willa Bentley was watching over Olivia's three-year-old son Aaron while Liv did her weekly Thursday-night bookkeeping job for the We Are One Church. As an accountant, she enjoyed working with numbers and it was the least she could do for the nice people who'd welcomed her with open arms.

Upon turning the corner, the hairs on the back of her neck rose in alarm. For the second time this week she had the distinct feeling she was being watched.

The Blake-Moore Group.

Was it possible the organization her late husband worked for had found her again, after all this time? Having overheard details about what the former soldiers belonging to the Blake-Moore Group had gotten involved in, she knew they were not to be trusted.

Resisting the urge to glance over her shoulder, she began to run, her movements awkward and clumsy because of her pregnant belly. Her oversize purse/diaper bag banged against her hip as she moved. The run didn't last long, and she slowed to a fast walk while frantically looking for someone nearby.

But there wasn't anyone around. For whatever reason, the streets of the Garden Ridge neighborhood were unusually vacant and quiet.

Liv pulled her phone from the front pocket of her bag, intending to call 911 despite her determination to avoid the police, but before she could push a button, large, strong hands roughly grabbed her from behind.

"No! Let me go!" She managed to get most of the words out mere seconds before a firm, calloused hand clamped hard over her mouth. Her phone fell uselessly to the ground with a loud clatter.

She couldn't breathe!

Panic flared, paralyzing her with fear. They'd found her. After all this time, the men employed by the Blake-Moore Group, the men who'd turned her husband into a monster, had found her!

Dear Lord, help me!

Desperate to save herself and her unborn baby, she lashed out against her attacker with all her strength, kicking backward with her feet and scratching at every exposed inch of skin on his face and hands.

"Knock it off," her attacker growled, his voice low and rough in her ear as his arm tightened painfully around her. "Or I'll kill you right here and now."

Kill her? No! This couldn't be happening! She thought about her son, Aaron, and her unborn baby. Her eyes burned with helpless tears as her attacker easily subdued her feeble struggles and began to pull her backward, away from the streetlights and deeper into the shadows.

She stopped struggling, in an attempt to preserve her strength while reminding herself that she'd escaped once before and could do so again. Granted, that was six months ago, when she'd only just discovered she was six weeks pregnant instead of thirty-four.

How had they found her?

"Oomph." The man holding her in his iron grasp abruptly let go. Still off-balance, Liv felt herself falling backward, even as she flailed her arms in an attempt to stay upright.

A pair of strong hands caught her before she could hit the ground, gently pushing her upright so that she was back on her own two feet. Her bag was somehow still on her shoulder and she hitched it higher, feeling relieved for a brief moment before realizing this could be another guy from the Blake-Moore Group.

"Let me go!" She shouted as loudly as she could, but the words came out like a weak croak. "Help! Police! Help me!"

"Olivia, please be quiet. We need to get out of here and pick up your son before this guy regains consciousness."

The stranger's use of her first name pulled her up short. She twisted out of his grasp and stared at his face, but he didn't look familiar. She noted he was dressed from head to toe in black, making it easy for him to blend into the night. Then her gaze dropped to the body of a man lying on the ground, also dressed in black, apparently unconscious. The silver glint of a knife blade lying on the asphalt beside him caught her eye, making her swallow hard.

What was going on? Who were these men?

"Olivia, I'm not with the Blake-Moore

Group," the stranger continued in a tone she was sure he meant to be reassuring. "I'm here to keep you and your son safe."

He knew about the Blake-Moore Group? And her son? Had he known her late husband, too? Questions flashed through her mind like laser beams, but she managed to pull out of his grasp, hitching her bag more securely over her shoulder then clutching the edges of her long blouse together like a shield over her belly.

She tucked a chin-length strand of dark hair behind her ear and bravely faced him. "I don't know who you are, but I'm fine on my own."

"You *were* fine on your own, until now," the stranger agreed. The fact that he didn't try to strong-arm her was confusing. She rubbed her hand over her belly, hoping he wouldn't notice her nervous gesture. "But there are likely others on the way. We need to leave immediately. We're running out of time."

She instinctively shook her head, not wanting to go, yet deep down she knew he was right. She and Aaron couldn't stay in Harrisburg any longer. Oddly enough, while they'd only been here for a little over two months, it already had begun to feel like home. Regret swelled in the back of her throat and it was all she could do to keep from bursting into tears.

Stupid hormones.

"My name is Ryker Tillman." In the darkness she couldn't see the stranger's facial features clearly, but noted he was taller than Tim had been, with broad shoulders and short dark hair. He cupped a hand beneath her elbow. "Come on—we need to hurry."

The name didn't mean anything to her and frankly she wasn't sure if that was good or bad. Ryker knew about the Blake-Moore Group, but claimed he wasn't one of them. But he hadn't said he was a cop, either.

Not that hearing he was a cop would have helped her relax. She'd trusted a cop once, but when he'd called the Blake-Moore Group, instead of backup, she'd realized he was in with them. Thankfully, she'd gotten away in time, and gone back on the run.

Nope, she wasn't doing that again.

"I don't know you and I don't trust you." She forced the words past her constricted throat. "Please leave me alone."

"I can't do that. They're obviously coming for you." Ryker urged her forward. "That guy was only the first. There will be more. Your son's nanny is this way, correct?"

Wait, he knew where Willa Bentley lived? Where she and Aaron lived? As much as she wanted to pull out of his grasp, she knew there was no possible way she could outrun him. For a moment she glanced back at the man lying on the sidewalk.

The assailant had threatened to kill her. Ryker Tillman claimed he wanted to protect her.

Why? What was this all about? She didn't know who or what to believe.

When she could see Willa's duplex up ahead, she began to doubt the wisdom of going along with this stranger. "You knew my husband, then? Timothy Habush?"

There was a momentary hesitation before Ryker spoke. "No, not personally. I knew of him, as we both served in Afghanistan. But he joined the Blake-Moore Group when we returned stateside while I decided to go in another direction."

To hear Ryker was former military wasn't surprising, and far from reassuring. She didn't want to be associated with another soldier. Her husband had once served with honor, but after his last tour of duty had ended, he'd decided to work for the Blake-Moore Group. After the first year, she'd known it was a mistake. The missions Tim had talked about were motivated by greed, not by doing what was right. When she'd overheard something about selling guns to the enemy, she'd felt sick at the realization Tim had sold out his country.

He'd sold out her, too. He'd been more interested in making money than having a family.

It had happened gradually, not all in one fell swoop. But one day, about a month before his death, she'd looked into his eyes and had seen nothing but a dull, flat emptiness.

His cold, dead eyes had scared her in a way nothing else ever had. Even now, the memory made her shiver.

She glanced up at the man at her side. It was too dark to see Ryker Tillman's eyes. Did they look the same way? Had being in combat changed him, the way it seemed to have changed her husband?

Tim was dead and so was her brother, Colin. It was all so surreal, especially when Colin had dragged her and Aaron out of the house during breakfast shortly before Christmas, insisting Tim wanted them to go into hiding. But it wasn't until she realized she and Aaron were locked in a small motel room that she understood they were being held prisoner under the guise of being safe.

Upon hearing the news that Tim was dead, she'd managed to escape Jeff, the guy Colin had ordered to watch over her. Oddly enough, the past several months being on her own with Aaron had felt liberating. Tim had become a coldhearted stranger to her, and when she'd discovered she was pregnant she'd worried about what her future, and the baby's future, would hold. As she left the Madison area, she told herself that it was better to be on her own. If Tim had lived, she felt certain he would have treated the new baby with the same indifference that he'd displayed toward Aaron.

On her own, she'd managed to drive Jeff's car to the closest town, then had been able to withdraw enough money from several ATMs. Her plan was to make her way south, seeking warmer weather. But her progress was slow. She'd stayed in one town for two weeks, the next town for three, the following one for two and so on. When she'd reached the charming town of Harrisburg, she'd liked it so much she'd decided to stay.

The two months she'd been here were wonderful. But now that the Blake-Moore Group had found her, the town was no longer safe.

She and Aaron would need to go on the run again.

As she walked down the street toward Willa's house, the feeling of dread became suffocating.

How in the world would she manage to keep running once her baby was born?

Ryker could tell Olivia's nerves were frayed and she was nearing her breaking point. There wasn't much time. They needed to get out of town. Maybe head into the Shawnee National Forest. It wouldn't be easy to hide off-grid considering Olivia's advanced pregnancy and her three-year-old son, but there wasn't another option.

The sooner they hit the road, the better.

He mentally kicked himself for letting that idiot get his hands on her in the first place. If he'd been quicker, he could have taken the guy out before he'd hurt her.

"I'm sorry." The words came out of his mouth before he could stop them. "I should have gotten to you sooner."

"You were following me?" The edge to her tone made him wince. But he wouldn't lie to her.

"Yes. But only because I'd noticed the guy from Blake-Moore following you." He'd been here for about two weeks, watching Olivia and her son from afar, shocked at first to discover she was very pregnant. He'd kept his distance, but then had gotten a glimpse of the mercenary following her.

The Blake-Moore Group was a team of former soldiers turned mercenaries who were highly paid to take on secret missions for anyone willing to fork up the asking price. In his opinion, they were motivated solely by greed, and that was enough to raise his suspicions.

About six months ago, he'd helped former army buddy Hawk Jacobson, his wife, Jillian, and their young daughter escape from the powerful man who'd hired the Blake-Moore Group to find and kill Hawk. Ryker had gladly helped arrest the man in charge and had assumed the group would have been disbanded.

But it seemed they were still afloat.

While helping Hawk with the investigation, he'd come across a scene at Tim Habush's house that had concerned him. A half-eaten breakfast, and the mysterious and obviously rushed disappearance of Olivia and Aaron.

His first priority was to help Hawk, but once that was finished, Ryker hadn't been able to get Olivia and Aaron out of his mind. It had bothered him that they were out there somewhere, likely scared and alone.

Vulnerable.

It hadn't been easy to find her; she'd done well staying under the radar. It had been frustrating to discover she'd disappeared without a trace. He'd backtracked, trying to ascertain what he'd missed, when he'd finally stumbled upon a clue. One of the last ATMs she'd used had been located near a small used-car lot outside Chicago. When he'd questioned the owner, the older guy denied knowing anything, but later that night, Ryker had entered the unlocked office and found paperwork that showed Olivia's car had been exchanged for an older model.

It was the break he'd been waiting for. With renewed vigor he'd gone back on the hunt, determined to find her. It had taken time, but that clue had finally led him here to Harrisburg, Illinois.

When he'd gotten his first glimpse of Olivia and Aaron, he'd felt a huge sense of relief to discover they were safe and unharmed. Yet he couldn't seem to simply walk away.

Especially once he'd realized Olivia was pregnant.

"Listen, Mr. Tillman," Olivia said as they walked up the short sidewalk toward the two-story house. "I really don't think—"

"Ryker. Please call me Ryker."

She let out an exasperated sound. "Ryker, then. I appreciate your willingness to help but Aaron and I can disappear easier on our own."

He didn't agree, but waited as she dug her key from the depths of a giant bag and inserted it into the lock. She opened the front door, and he followed her inside.

"Willa? I'm home," she called.

The interior of the house seemed unusually quiet. From the little interaction he'd had with Hawk's daughter Lizzie, he knew young kids tended to make noise.

"Willa?" There was a note of worry in Olivia's tone.

He pulled his weapon, just in case. "What is it?" he asked in a low voice.

"She usually waits up for me."

There was a light on in the kitchen, but the rest of the lower-level apartment was dark.

Every one of his senses went on full alert.

Something was very wrong.

"Stay behind me." Ryker gently but firmly pushed Olivia behind him. He debated whether or not to tell Olivia to call the police, but decided to find out what they were dealing with first.

"Where is Aaron's room?" he asked in a whisper.

"His room is upstairs next to mine," she whispered back.

He nodded and made his way down the short hallway to the two bedrooms separated by a tiny bathroom. One bedroom door was open, the other was closed.

With his foot, he shoved the door hanging ajar all the way open. The room was apparently used as a guest room and appeared empty.

Behind him, Olivia sucked in a harsh breath and he knew she hadn't expected the room to be vacant. He took a moment to check the closet and beneath the bed, before deeming the room clear.

He checked the bathroom next, but found nothing.

Testing the knob of the closed bedroom door, he found it wasn't locked. Keeping Olivia behind him, he abruptly shoved the door open, then stepped back to wait.

Nothing happened. Leading with his weapon, Ryker cautiously crossed the threshold, then stopped abruptly when he saw the older woman lying on the bed.

After checking in the closet and beneath the bed to make sure there wasn't anyone hiding in wait, he crossed over to feel for a pulse.

The nanny was dead.

"Willa!" Olivia's horrified gasp indicated she knew the woman was gone. "Oh no! Where's Aaron?"

"Olivia, please," he tried but then he heard the sound of someone coming down the stairs. "Run away and call for help."

"Not without my son!" She had her phone in her hand, but he knew any chance of help arriving would be too late.

"Go!" He pushed Olivia toward the door then quickly but silently crossed the living room into the kitchen, flipping the light off as he went.

There was a side doorway that he felt certain led up to the second-story apartment.

He took up a defensive position behind the door, and waited, hoping the guy who likely had Aaron didn't know that his cohort in crime had failed at kidnapping Olivia.

"Mommy! Mommy! I want my Mommy!" Aaron's cries echoed high and shrill above the thumping footsteps coming down the stairs.

"Aaron! I'm here, baby, don't worry!" Olivia's voice rang out loudly and Ryker momentarily closed his eyes, wishing he'd handled things differently.

He should have gotten Olivia and Aaron out of the city the moment he'd found them.

Instead he may cause the very thing he'd been trying to avoid.

Getting them both killed.

The footsteps came closer and he instantly felt all his emotions drain away, a sense of cool calmness washing over him. Every one of his senses was keenly focused on the threat and what needed to be done.

The same eerie sense of control had always come over him when he faced death. Back in Afghanistan and back in December while he'd been helping Hawk.

From his position he could see that Olivia hadn't left the duplex as ordered. He speared her with a stern look, but she ignored him. At least she was hovering near the doorway leading into the kitchen, somewhat protected behind the wall.

Except for her pregnant belly which was too large to hide.

He waved her back, but Olivia didn't see him. Her eyes were glued to the doorway.

Steeling his resolve to get her and the boy out of this mess, he waited.

"Mommy, Mommy!" Aaron cried again. "Lemme go!"

Ryker sensed the man holding Olivia's son was standing on the other side of the doorway, planning his next move. Ryker believed the perp was cowardly enough to use the child as a shield.

Which meant he'd have to find a way to take the guy out without harming the little boy.

His gut knotted with tension, but he kept his ears and eyes focused on the door. Ignoring the child's cries wasn't easy, but then he heard the barest whisper of sound.

He dropped his gaze to the doorknob and watched it slowly and silently turn. He mentally counted the seconds.

The door flew open. There was a long pause but Ryker was ready. He shot out from behind the door, bringing his gun hand down hard on the back of the perp's head.

"No! Aaron!" Olivia cried.

The guy stumbled, but didn't go down or let go of the child. Ryker grabbed his shoulder and hit him again just as Olivia rushed forward and grabbed for Aaron.

On some level he was aware of Olivia wrenching Aaron out of the perp's grasp, even as the big guy groaned and turned toward Ryker. In a nanosecond Ryker saw the gun and fired.

The sound of twin gunshots echoed loudly through the kitchen, and a flash of pain along the upper part of his left leg made Ryker realize he'd been hit.

But he forced himself to ignore it. They had to move! Keeping Olivia and her son safe was all that mattered.

TWO

"Ryker!" Poised near the front doorway, Liv hesitated. She wasn't sure why she was suddenly so worried about the stranger she hadn't trusted a few minutes ago, but she couldn't bear to leave him behind.

The man who'd had Aaron collapsed on the floor at Ryker's feet. He groaned but didn't move. Bright red blood began to pool beside him on the floor.

"Go! I'm right behind you." Ryker staggered forward, carefully stepping around the man. "We need to get out of here before the cops arrive."

Logically she knew they shouldn't leave the scene of a crime. They should wait for the police. But she'd been on the run for so long, she couldn't do it. Hiking Aaron higher in her arms, she followed Ryker outside. Willa was dead and two men had almost succeeded in grabbing her and Aaron.

Every fiber of her being longed to get far away from the quaint town she'd once thought could be her new home.

"This way." Ryker once again cupped his hand beneath her elbow, guiding her to the left.

"Wait." She dug in her heels. "I have a car here."

"No good. That's how they tracked you. I have a vehicle stashed on the next block."

They'd tracked her here through her car? How was that possible? She'd exchanged her newer car for an older model and asked the owner of the used-car lot to keep the transaction off the books.

"How do you know that?" she asked, already feeling breathless. Aaron wasn't overly big for his age, but she was carrying her unborn baby, as well. She'd tried to keep in shape, but obviously she wasn't going to be able to continue going at this pace for long.

"Because that's how I found you." Ryker glanced down at her. "Will Aaron cry if I hold him? We need to hurry."

"Yes, he's likely to cry, since the man on the stairs scared him." The little boy was calmer now, but was sucking his thumb, a habit he'd broken six months ago. He was also, thankfully, wearing a Pull-Ups diaper as she could tell he'd wet himself.

The poor child had been scared to death.

She tried to match Ryker's long-legged stride to avoid slowing them down. But seconds later, she could hear the wail of sirens.

"Almost there," Ryker said encouragingly as he continued urging her forward. "See the black SUV?"

"Yes." She was breathless with exertion, but pushed herself to keep going. It wasn't until they reached his car that she realized they didn't have a car seat for Aaron.

"Wait! We need a car seat," she protested when Ryker opened the passenger door for her.

"I already have one in the back, see? Let me strap him in." Without asking permission, he plucked Aaron from her arms and opened the back door to place the toddler in his safety seat.

Amazingly, Aaron didn't cry. She wondered if her son sensed they were safe with Ryker.

It wasn't until she'd climbed in and buckled her seat belt and Ryker slid in behind the wheel that the significance of the child safety seat hit her.

"You were planning to take me and Aaron all along!" Betrayal hit hard and she fumbled for the door handle. "You're one of them! I can't believe I fell for your act and—"

"Don't, Olivia." Ryker's voice wasn't harsh, but firm. "I have never lied to you. I don't work for the Blake-Moore Group, in fact I helped bring some of their men down. However, I have been trying to find you and Aaron to make sure you were safe. That's why I have a car seat. I wanted to be ready if they came for you."

He'd already pulled away from the curb and was driving slowly away from Willa's home. Liv glanced at her purse/diaper bag, thinking about the clothing and toys she'd left behind, and bit down on her lower lip to keep from crying.

Were they really safe with Ryker? She wanted to trust her instincts, but too much had happened in such a short time. Her life as she'd known it was over.

It had first ended six months ago, and now for a second time, as well. How many new starts could she handle?

How many could Aaron handle?

"Listen, I know you have no reason to trust me," Ryker said calmly. "But I've been worried about you and Aaron for months. Since a few days before Christmas when I was at your house and realized you and your son had been removed in a hurry."

She glanced over at him, wishing she could see his eyes. But the interior of the car was too dark.

"I'm sorry your husband and brother are dead," he continued. "But you need to know they were attempting to kill a friend of mine, leaving us no choice but to stop them."

She stiffened in her seat as the realization sank deep. "You killed Tim and Colin?"

"Technically, my buddy killed your husband in self-defense," he corrected. "But yes, I'm sorry to say I had a part in killing your brother. Just know, I only did it to save my friend Hawk's life."

He wasn't telling her anything she hadn't suspected, but the news sent her reeling all the same.

Ryker had killed her brother. The older brother she'd once looked up to. She and Colin had been close once, but that was before he'd done a tour overseas.

Before he'd joined the Blake-Moore Group.

Before he'd turned into a killer.

On some level she was surprised Ryker was being so bluntly honest with her. He easily could have kept that information to himself.

"Why?" The word came out low and strained.

"I told you, to save my friend's life. And I only fired in self-defense."

"No, why were my husband and brother going after your friend?"

There was a long pause before Ryker answered. "The Blake-Moore Group was hired by a man high up in the government to silence

Hawk because he knew too much about the guy's role in illegal arms dealing. They sold American guns to the enemy."

She closed her eyes as shame washed over her. To have her own flesh and blood and the father of her children involved in what was little more than a murder-for-hire scheme made her sick. She had to take several deep breaths to keep from throwing up in Ryker's car.

Wishing she'd brought some crackers along, she waited for the nausea to pass. When she opened her eyes, she was startled to realize they were already outside the city limits.

"Where are we going?"

"South." Ryker's answer wasn't helpful.

"Where, south? What city?"

This time he didn't respond for several long moments. She was about to ask again, when he said, "I thought we'd hide out in the Shawnee National Forest for what's left of the night and decide where to go from there in the morning."

Liv glanced over her shoulder at Aaron, who'd fallen asleep. "I can't stay in the forest with Aaron. It's too remote. He's never camped outside."

"They have hotels," Ryker said dryly. "There are cabins for rent, too."

"Oh." She felt foolish for assuming the worst. Rubbing a hand over her belly, she did her best to remain calm. Being upset and anxious wasn't good for the baby.

"How far along are you?" Ryker asked.

"Thirty-four weeks. I'm due in six weeks." She frowned. "I'll need to establish care with a new obstetrician soon, though. Since I can't go back to the one I was seeing in Harrisburg."

"Of course."

She felt an odd comfort in knowing that if anything did happen to her, Ryker seemed to be the kind of guy to get her and the baby the help they'd need.

Maybe between God and Ryker, she and Aaron would be okay.

Ryker thought about calling his buddy Duncan O'Hare for help. He'd have called Hawk, but knew Hawk had taken his family on a honeymoon/vacation to Florida. Duncan would help, but Ryker decided to wait. No doubt he would soon need the assistance of others, but for now he just wanted to get Olivia and Aaron settled somewhere safe.

The side of his left leg burned like crazy, but he knew the bullet had only grazed him. The wound wasn't bad enough to slow him down. He figured there would be time later to examine the injury.

His instinct was to use one of the cabin motels. From the research he'd done online, the cabins in the Shawnee forest were spread out from each other creating a better sense of isolation than what he and Hawk had experienced before Christmas.

He cast a sidelong look at Olivia. She appeared to be resting, her palms spread protectively over her belly. He had a picture of Olivia and Aaron that he'd taken from her home tucked deep in his pocket, but the photo didn't do her justice.

She was heart-stoppingly beautiful. Her dark hair was cut shorter than what she'd worn in the photo, but he liked the way the ends curved along the edge of her jaw.

Wait a minute. He gave himself a mental shake. There was no point in thinking about how pretty she was, or how cute Aaron looked sucking his thumb. The last thing he wanted was a relationship. Not after the way he'd lost his girlfriend and her young daughter in a senseless carjacking while he'd been deployed overseas. He never wanted to feel that kind of sorrow again, yet couldn't help but reach out to help women and children in danger.

The way he'd wished others had helped his girlfriend and her daughter.

Besides, Olivia was mourning the loss of her

husband and brother, and he'd been personally involved in their deaths, in a big way.

He hadn't shied away from telling her about his role in their deaths. He didn't want to lie to her, yet he hadn't exactly told her the entire truth. There was no good reason for her to know that her brother had held a gun to Jillian's head while threatening to kill her and her four-year-old daughter, Lizzie.

Ryker always felt remorse when he was forced to shoot someone, even knowing that the deed had been done to save the lives of innocents. It was the main reason he had only done one tour in the army. Being deployed in Afghanistan had been difficult. For one thing he'd left his girlfriend and her daughter behind, along with his foster parents. But more so because of the seemingly endless violence.

And here he was tangled up with another case that forced him to use skills he'd rather forget he possessed.

The close call at the nanny's house had sent a cold chill down the back of his neck. He and the perp had both fired their weapons at nearly the exact same time but thankfully Ryker had had the advantage.

If not, the outcome would have been much different.

He rubbed a weary hand over his face and focused on taking less-traveled highways to reach the Shawnee National Forest. When he came up to the gate, he pulled out his wallet and rolled down his window.

"Good evening," he greeted the guy at the gate. He sensed Olivia was awake, but she kept her eyes closed. "We'd like a week-long pass. We're spending some time at the Cedar Rock Cabins."

The guy nodded and took the cash Ryker offered in exchange for a seven-day pass. He slid it in the lower-left-hand corner of the windshield so it was visible to the rangers, and then drove through the gate.

When they'd cleared the area, Olivia straightened. "You have this all planned out, don't you?" Her accusatory tone caught him off guard.

"Not exactly. I mean I know about the Cedar Rock Cabins, but we don't have a reservation. I'm hoping they aren't booked."

"And if they are?"

"Then we'll keep going until we find a place to stay." He glanced over at her. "I won't make you and Aaron sleep in the car. We'll find something."

She let out a sigh and relaxed. "Okay, sorry. All of this seems so crazy. I keep thinking of Willa. She didn't deserve this. I hate knowing her death is my fault. I just don't understand why the Blake-Moore Group is going to such lengths to get me back."

The idea had bothered him, too. He'd been focused on finding Olivia and Aaron, but he didn't really understand why she was in danger. His instincts had been right, but he had no idea why they wanted her.

"You really don't know why they're after you?" He tried to sound nonchalant, even though he'd always suspected she knew why she was in danger.

"No. I've thought back over those last few months before things got so crazy." She grimaced and rubbed her stomach again. "I hadn't seen much of Tim during that time, and when Colin showed up that day, dragging me and Aaron out of the house, I knew something was wrong."

He found that information rather curious. "Your brother didn't tell you why you had to leave in such a rush?"

"He only said that we were in danger." Her tone was defensive. "But after twenty-four hours I could tell the guy watching over us was getting nervous. I heard him talking on the phone, that's how I learned Tim had been killed. That concerned me, but when I asked about Colin, the guy told me he'd be there soon, but I felt certain he was lying. That Colin was dead, just like Tim. Then I discovered the door was locked from the outside, which only heightened my feeling that something was wrong. The guy was basically keeping us prisoners in that dive of a motel room and I started to think that it might be on orders from someone higher up at Blake-Moore. At that moment, I decided that it might be best to go off on our own."

"You escaped?"

"Yep. Told Jeff I was pregnant and bleeding. He panicked and when he turned to call his boss, I hit him over the head with a lamp and took his car keys." There was a note of pride in her voice.

His lips curved in a smile. "Good for you."

"I thought I did a good job of getting away without leaving a trail." The confidence in her tone faded. "But I was wrong."

"Hey." He reached over to take her hand. "Don't sell yourself short. It's not every woman who could escape former military special ops guys for six months. If it wasn't for the paperwork I found at the used-car lot, I wouldn't have found you. And neither would anyone from the Blake-Moore Group."

"I told that guy not to keep the paperwork!" She sounded angry now. "He promised he'd shred it. Claimed he knew someone who'd take the car off his hands even without the title."

"You should have made him shred the documents while you watched." Ryker wasn't sure why he was giving her advice on how to stay under the radar. She didn't need it now that he was there to watch over her. "But it doesn't matter now. You, Aaron and the baby are safe."

"For now." He hated hearing the faint note of hopelessness in her tone.

"For as long as I'm alive," he swiftly corrected. "And I have friends who will help us if needed. You'll never be alone."

He could feel her gaze on him, but kept his eyes on the winding road weaving through the dense foliage.

A faint rumbling from her stomach caught his attention. "You hungry?"

She looked embarrassed as she rubbed her belly.

The corner of his mouth kicked up in a reluctant smile. Ryker knew he should have thought of food earlier. "There are plenty of places to get food around here. Just let me know what you're in the mood for."

As the words left his mouth, they came upon a sign advertising Torra Tacos one mile ahead.

"Maybe something less spicy," she said. "Heartburn has been my constant companion over the past few weeks."

"There's a burger joint in five miles. Will that work?"

Her answer was another rumble coming from her stomach which made his smile widen.

Ryker had to respect the way she'd taken everything in stride. The sign for the Cedar Rock Cabins indicated they were located about twelve miles away, so stopping for food wasn't a problem. He thought about getting breakfast, too, something they could easily heat up for Aaron in the morning.

He pulled up to the drive-through window and looked expectantly at Olivia. She was intently scanning the menu before placing her order for a cheeseburger and a bottle of water.

The restaurant didn't offer breakfast at this hour, so he settled for getting several burgers to go, knowing that having some food was better than nothing at all.

"You're going to eat four burgers all by yourself?"

"No, just one. The others can be warmed up in the morning." He paid for the food, then handed the bag to Olivia.

Thankfully, they got a cabin, one that was located in a secluded area off the main road. Ryker was glad to have four-wheel drive as he headed up the rugged hill.

He was relieved to find the cabin was clean

and had indoor plumbing. Olivia brought the bag of food in, then went back out to get Aaron. The little boy didn't wake up as she carried him inside.

While she was busy, Ryker quickly ducked into the bathroom to examine his thigh wound, grateful to realize it wasn't bad. When he emerged, he found Olivia pulling a fresh diaper from the bag. She went back and changed Aaron, before gently placing him on one of the twin beds and pulling the covers up over his pajamas.

She was a good mother. Not like his who'd abandoned him at the age of ten. Ryker pushed the unwelcome thoughts away. He unpacked her cheeseburger and his Quarter Pounder at the kitchen table. When Olivia returned she washed her hands, then removed her large purse from her shoulder and set it on the table. Then she surprised him by crossing over to where he was seated. She stood over him and cupped her hands on either side of his face.

The soft touch of her fingers made him go still. Her blue eyes, clear as the sea, stared into his.

"What's wrong?" He barely recognized his own voice.

She stared down at him intently for a long moment before releasing him. "Nothing. I just wanted to see your eyes."

"My eyes?" He missed the warmth of her hands, wondering if she had something against hazel-colored eyes.

"Yes." She pulled a chair from the table and sat down. "I needed to see for myself."

"See what?" He couldn't hide his bafflement.

"I needed to see exactly who I am about to trust with my life, my son's life and that of my unborn child." She avoided his gaze now as she picked up her cheeseburger and took a bite.

He shook his head, battling confusion. What had she seen in his eyes? He had no idea, but decided to let it go.

Mostly because he'd liked the brush of her fingers on his skin a little too much. He had to resist the urge to touch the same spot her fingers had been.

Idiot. Olivia wasn't Cheri, and Aaron was hardly little Cyndi. He wasn't going down the path of caring too much. He sternly reminded himself that his role was only to keep Olivia, her baby and Aaron safe.

Getting emotionally and personally involved wasn't an option.

THREE

Ryker's hazel eyes were alive, full of caring, compassion and concern.

He wasn't the type of man her husband and brother had turned into and for that she was grateful.

Yet it was pretty clear he was a soldier. The way he'd taken out the bad guy holding Aaron had left no doubt about that. She was touched by the fact that he hadn't outright killed him, firing only because the other guy had. And she was especially grateful that he hadn't been injured in the struggle.

The cheeseburger congealed in her stomach. She took a deep breath. Those minutes inside Willa's house had been the scariest of her entire life.

Worse than being attacked on the street by that guy from Blake-Moore. Hearing Aaron's cries, seeing that stranger gripping her son with that harsh look in his eyes, had been heart-wrenching. And poor Willa. Her eyes filled. Willa had never hurt anyone and hadn't deserved to die.

"Olivia, don't." Ryker reached out and lightly touched the back of her hand. "Don't dwell on what nearly happened back there. Concentrate on your future. Reliving that fear and worry can't be good for the baby, right?"

His kindness only made her eyes burn with more tears as she tried to smile. "Right."

Ryker gestured to her meal. "Eat up. I'm sure the baby is hungry."

Taking another bite of her burger, she did her best to ignore the weird awareness that had come out of nowhere when she'd held Ryker's face and looked deep into his hazel eyes.

Ridiculous to be attracted to a man who was only trying to help her out of a dangerous situation. She was as big as an ox and would only get bigger as the baby grew. No man would be interested in someone who probably not only outweighed him but waddled when she walked.

Besides, she wasn't about to become involved with him. With any man, but especially not another soldier. The last few weeks of her marriage to Tim had been difficult. She'd known Tim since high school; he'd always been Colin's best friend. Tim was a man she'd known for ten years, yet somehow her husband of five years had turned into a complete stranger.

If that sort of personality change could happen to Tim, it could happen to anyone. She was better off alone, especially since she would have her hands full with a new baby to care for.

These feelings stirring deep within must be gratitude toward Ryker, nothing more. Not only had he saved her life, but he'd helped rescue Aaron. Despite her earlier misgivings, she was thankful that he'd come to find her.

She risked another glance at him from beneath her lashes. Ryker was handsome. His chiseled features belonged on billboards selling anything that women might want to buy. Even something they didn't want to buy, but would anyway once they saw him. Yet she still found it odd that he'd come all this way to find her and Aaron just because he'd feared they were in danger.

Who did that? Who jumped at the chance to get involved in a perilous situation to protect strangers? She had no idea.

It wasn't until she finished her meal that she remembered she'd forgotten to pray. Attending church with Willa these past few weeks had been amazing, but she still wasn't used to doing the simple things like thanking God for her food. She sent up a quick, silent, guilty prayer then crumpled up her empty wrapper and pushed to her feet.

"I'll take that." Ryker plucked the garbage from her hand while pressing on her arm. "Just sit and relax, okay?"

She sank back down into her seat, eyeing him warily. "Don't worry, I don't think all of this excitement will send me into early labor."

The flash of frank fear in his gaze was oddly reassuring. "Don't joke about that."

Her smile faded and she rubbed her hands over her belly. "You're right—it's not a laughing matter. I want this baby to keep growing inside for as long as possible. My doctor says the baby shouldn't come much before forty weeks."

Ryker scrubbed his palms over his face for a moment and she could tell the responsibility of keeping her, Aaron and the baby safe had overwhelmed him.

She liked that he cared about her, and about the baby she carried. Her instincts told her Ryker was a man she could trust.

Of course, she'd once felt that way about Tim and look where that had gotten her.

She tried not to remember the way their marriage had slowly unraveled over time. Like a sweater, first the hem, then the sleeves then finally the entire garment until there was nothing left but a pile of yarn.

"Would you like some herbal tea?" He held up a box of chamomile tea that must have been left behind by previous occupants of the cabin. "There isn't a microwave but I can heat some water on the stove."

"That would be nice." Liv knew that she'd need to sit and relax for a while before trying to sleep. She pulled her purse toward her and rummaged for the bottle of antacids she kept with her at all times. No matter how dull and bland the food was, the baby pushed up on her stomach in a way that caused endless heartburn.

"Are you certain you don't know why the men of the Blake-Moore Group are after you?"

She glanced up at Ryker, who was leaning against the counter with his arms crossed over his chest. A small pan of water was heating on the stove, but he looked anything but domestic standing there. The gun on his hip and the muscles straining at his shirtsleeves made her mouth go dry.

Stop it! She gave herself a mental shake and did her best to concentrate on what was important. "I've been thinking about that since I first went on the run," she admitted. "But honestly, I can't think of anything that would make anyone within the organization upset with me."

Ryker's gaze was steady. "Have you met the owners? Harper Moore or Kevin Blake?"

She frowned, thinking back to when Tim had first talked about his new job. He'd spoken of the two men, but had she met them? There had been a welcome-to-the-group party early on with other members of the Blake-Moore organization, and she thought maybe Kevin Blake and Harper Moore had been there. But for the life of her, she couldn't bring either man's face into focus.

"About four years ago," she admitted. "But I met a lot of guys Tim worked with back then, and I can't say for sure who was who. I vaguely remember being introduced to the owners during the Fourth of July barbecue."

"Nothing more recent?" Ryker pressed.

"No. Those gatherings didn't last. Things changed within the first year Tim was with them. I originally thought it was because of Aaron and the fact that Tim hadn't adjusted well to having a baby disrupting our lives. But over time, I got the sense that the camaraderie between the men had changed. At least as far as Tim was concerned. It seemed to be more competitive. He slowly became someone I could barely recognize." She felt a little guilty for speaking poorly of her husband. Of Aaron's and the baby's father. She smoothed her hand over her abdomen, trying not to imagine how incredibly difficult it would be to raise two children on her own.

If Willa was here, she'd remind Liv that she would never be alone as long as she had faith in God. She clung to the memory of the woman who'd loved her like a mother. Who'd treated Aaron like a grandmother would.

A sense of fierceness washed over her. She wanted the men who'd killed Willa to pay for their crimes.

Ryker set a steaming cup of tea before her and she thankfully cupped her hands around it, savoring the warmth.

"It just doesn't make sense." She shook her head, feeling helpless. "I've tried to think of what could have happened to cause Tim's bosses to come after me, but I can't think of anything."

"It's okay." Ryker offered a lopsided smile. "I don't want you to stress about it. For now, all that matters is that you and Aaron are safe."

She took a sip of her tea, enjoying the calming scent. "Thanks to you, Ryker."

A shadow crossed his features. "No reason to thank me," he said in a low voice. "I should have acted sooner."

She tipped her head, regarding him thoughtfully. "You were the one who told me not to dwell on what happened back there, but to focus on the future. Maybe you should consider taking your own advice."

A ghost of a smile flitted across his features. "Maybe."

Liv finished the rest of her tea and set the mug aside. "Thanks again, Ryker. For everything."

This time he accepted her gratitude. He tipped his head in a nod. "Get some rest. We'll likely have to find a new place to stay in the morning."

The idea of leaving so soon bothered her, but she didn't argue. Pushing up from her seat, she winced at the sore muscles in her legs. Running was not a normal activity for her these days. She carried her mug to the sink then turned and glanced back over her shoulder.

"Good night."

"Good night, Olivia."

She used the bathroom first, chewed another antacid, then slipped silently into the room she shared with Aaron.

A wave of exhaustion hit hard. Moments before she fell asleep, she found herself secretly wishing that Tim could have been half the man Ryker seemed to be.

Ryker waited until Olivia was safely tucked in with her son before heading into the bathroom to further tend to his wound. He was glad that his black jeans had hidden the oozing blood.

The gash was long and jagged, but superficial. He cleaned the wound and, since there were no bandages in the medicine cabinet, ended up wrapping a clean towel around his thigh. Then he washed the blood from his jeans.

In his room, he laid the jeans out near a window, hoping they'd dry by morning.

He stretched out on the bed, but knew sleep wouldn't come easily. As a soldier he'd learned to fall asleep in two minutes or less, but that was easier to do when you only had to worry about yourself and when your team consisted of capable soldiers.

Knowing that there were three lives in the other room depending on him was enough to have him staring wide-eyed at the ceiling, his heart thudding heavily in his chest.

He really didn't want Olivia to go into premature labor. The best way to do that was to stay three steps ahead of the Blake-Moore Group.

Duncan O'Hare would help, as would any of the Callahans. Mike, Marc, Mitch, Matthew and Miles Callahan were all brothers, and their sister Maddy was married to Noah, who was also a cop. One of them should be able to help. Hawk, too, if he wasn't on vacation. Ryker decided he'd call Duncan and Mike Callahan once they'd moved to a new location.

Feeling better about his plan, he tried to relax, yet thoughts whirled through his head. It was strange that Olivia had no idea why the Blake-Moore mercenaries had come after her. But he found himself believing her when she claimed to be in the dark.

He'd helped Hawk and the Feds arrest Todd Hayes, the former secretary of defense, for selling illegal guns to the enemy in Afghanistan. Hayes had hired the Blake-Moore Group, specifically Colin Yonkers and Tim Habush, to find and kill Hawk because he'd seen too much and because they'd both been involved in the gun selling.

With Hayes being held in a federal prison, it didn't make sense that the Blake-Moore Group was still intact, much less that they'd come after Olivia.

Somehow, he managed to sleep, because the next thing he knew, bright sunlight was streaming in through the window. His wound was still raw and prone to bleeding, but he tossed the towel on the floor and pulled on his still damp jeans. When there was time and everyone was safe, he'd find a place to get bandages.

He stared dubiously at the cold burgers he'd purchased sitting on a shelf in the otherwise empty fridge. Without a microwave, they would taste awful. He decided to head to the closest restaurant that served breakfast instead.

Aaron would be hungry, and so would Olivia.

There was a coffeepot and just enough grounds left in a small can to make a half of a carafe, so he made coffee, then went outside to his SUV to get his laptop. No reason he couldn't start working while he waited for Olivia and Aaron to get up.

Sipping his coffee, Ryker focused on the computer screen. His phone indicated less than a fifty percent charge on the battery, but he had a charger in the SUV, so he didn't hesitate to use it as a hot spot for his computer.

The Blake-Moore Group's website hadn't been updated or changed in any way since the last time he'd checked. He did another search on both Kevin Blake and Harper Moore, but knew that both men were experts at staying off-grid.

He tried to think of another way to figure out who Blake or Moore had sent to pick up Olivia. The way the man had grabbed and dragged her backward on the street, while the other one had grabbed Aaron, led him to believe they hadn't been sent to outright kill either of them.

Not until they had whatever it was they wanted.

But what?

A physical item? He rolled the idea over in his mind. With Olivia on the run it didn't make sense that she'd have anything of value on her person. No, it must be a memory. Something she knew that must be important.

But Olivia said she didn't know anything. Didn't understand why Blake-Moore had come after her. How would they figure out what it was the mercenaries wanted?

The whole thing made his head hurt.

Ryker tried another angle, checking on some of the companies who'd provided reviews about the great work the Blake-Moore Group had done for them. As he scanned the reviews, he read about a hostage rescue the Blake-Moore Group had performed roughly four years ago.

It was old news, but he couldn't help but wonder if this was one of the first missions Olivia's husband had done. He remembered how she'd mentioned the Fourth of July celebration and how there had once been a lot of camaraderie. It made sense if they were celebrating their success.

They'd been a legitimate group once; the hostage rescue proved that. But something had changed over time. Maybe it had been taking on Todd Hayes as a client. Maybe they'd started with lower-level government workers and had eventually proved themselves worthy.

Yet he knew Colin Yonkers had played a role in selling guns to the enemy. It was possible that Tim hadn't realized how far Colin had gotten into trouble until it was too late.

He straightened in his seat. What if Tim had confided in Olivia? Could be that he shared something he shouldn't have.

"I hav'ta go potty." Aaron's young voice coming from the living room drew him from his dark thoughts.

"This way, sweetie." Olivia took her son's hand and led him to the bathroom.

Ryker quickly turned off the computer and tucked it into Olivia's large bag. He put his phone in his pocket, making a note to charge it once they were in the SUV. He finished his coffee, then quickly washed the cup and replaced it in the cupboard.

As soon as Olivia and Aaron were finished in the bathroom, it would be time to hit the road. They weren't that far from Nashville, but he'd also considered heading north to where he knew Duncan O'Hare and the Callahan family were located.

The Blake-Moore Group wouldn't expect them to double back the way they'd come.

He wasn't sure Olivia would like that idea, but having others available to help watch over her and Aaron was more important than staying hidden in the forest.

Olivia and Aaron emerged from the bathroom fifteen minutes later. She crossed over to take her bag, surprised to find the laptop in there.

"Sorry, but I thought it would be easier for me to carry it from now on," he explained.

"I just need a change of clothes for Aaron. He wants to wear big-boy undies." She set the laptop aside and rummaged around for what she needed, then replaced the computer.

"We need to leave," he reminded her. "We can stop for breakfast on the way."

"This will only take a minute." She took Aaron over to the sofa and managed to get the squirmy boy into clean clothes.

"Ready?" He took the discarded pajamas from her and stuffed them into the bag, before looping the strap over his shoulder.

"You know that's basically a glorified diaper bag, right?" She held out a hand. "I'll carry it."

"I don't mind." The surprise in her eyes made him wonder if her husband hadn't liked carrying the black-and-white zebra-striped bag. He didn't understand what the big deal was. Besides, adding the laptop made the bag heavy. Better for him to shoulder the burden. "Let's go."

He followed her and Aaron outside. The sun

was nice, but would grow impossibly warm as the day went on.

Olivia buckled Aaron in his car seat, while he set the bag on the floor of the passenger-side seat. Within minutes they were on the road.

"Why are we going back the way we came?" Olivia asked.

"There was a family restaurant I thought would be a good place to have breakfast." He knew he'd have to discuss his plan to head north in more detail soon.

"I was thinking the fast-food restaurant we used last night would be better. I remember seeing a play area for Aaron." She glanced at him. "Their breakfast sandwiches are decent."

"Sure, why not?" He was more than willing to make her happy. After several miles, he turned into the parking lot. He parked off to the opposite side of the building from where the play area was located.

The restaurant was situated near the base of a mountain with a hiking trail that led down to a tree-laden ravine. Ryker looped the diaper bag over his shoulder, then swept his gaze over the area, scanning for anything out of the ordinary.

There was nothing suspicious, so they went inside and ordered their breakfast. They chose a table in the back, near the indoor play area.

Aaron drank his chocolate milk in ten seconds flat, then wanted to go down the slide.

"Go ahead," Olivia said. "You can eat your breakfast bagel in the car."

Ryker had only taken a few bites of his breakfast sandwich when he caught a glimpse of a black SUV with tinted windows driving past the restaurant. It slowed dramatically, causing the driver behind it to lay on the horn.

A warning chill snaked over him. He instantly stood and stuffed his meal back into the wrapper and tucked it in the bag. "Get Aaron. We need to go."

"Go where?" Olivia turned to follow his gaze, then went pale. She stashed her sandwich with his, then rose to her feet looking for her son. "Aaron!"

"Wheee!" The little boy was laughing with glee as he came down the slide.

Ryker shouldered the oversize bag, then crossed over to get Aaron. Thankfully, the boy didn't cry, but wiggled around impatiently. "No. I wanna go down the slide."

Ryker ignored him. "This way." He headed toward the back door of the restaurant.

Outside, he could see the path going down to the ravine. He debated for a moment, then realized that if the Blake-Moore mercenaries had run his license plate, the vehicle wasn't safe.

"We're heading down the path," he whispered.

To her credit, Olivia didn't complain, but led the way down the winding trail. He worried she might fall, so he didn't rush her despite his instincts screaming that they needed to hurry.

Two car doors slammed loudly. From this angle, he couldn't see his vehicle, but imagined that the two men would check his SUV first, before going inside the restaurant. Precious seconds that they needed in order to stay ahead of them.

He and Olivia continued down the path dropping out of sight from the restaurant, but it wouldn't be long before the mercenaries realized they were on foot and likely on the hiking trail.

Escaping two armed men without a set of wheels would be impossible. He was armed, but they would have double the firepower.

Dread tightened his chest, making it difficult to breathe. Once again, he'd waited too long to call for backup and had put their lives in jeopardy.

FOUR

Her heart thundered so loudly she was surprised Ryker didn't hear it. Maneuvering down the dirt path wasn't easy because she couldn't see her feet over her stomach. The only reason she was able to move quickly was because Ryker was carrying both her bag and Aaron.

"Where are we going?" Aaron asked.

"Shh. Be quiet. We're playing a game of hide-and-seek." Ryker's attempt to keep her son silent was genius.

To be honest, she hadn't seen anything suspicious when Ryker had rushed them out of the fast-food restaurant. But once they'd gotten outside, she'd heard two car doors slamming shut. Two men? Like the two who'd come after her and Aaron in Harrisburg? She swallowed hard, horrified at the idea of more men coming after them, yet she was extremely thankful she wasn't alone.

She firmly believed God had sent Ryker to keep her and Aaron safe.

How in the world had the Blake-Moore Group found them again? They weren't that far from Harrisburg, yet she couldn't begin to understand how they'd tracked her and Ryker to the fast-food place.

Except, Ryker hadn't killed the man who'd grabbed her on the street; he'd only knocked him out. Could the assailant have regained consciousness long enough to watch them escape in Ryker's SUV? Had he somehow used the license plate to track them down? She knew from first-hand experience that the Blake-Moore Group had connections within law enforcement.

Her right foot slipped on a rock, sending her reeling off-balance. Her weight shifted and she teetered for a long second, her arms flailing, knowing she was going to fall. Ryker's hand shot out, grabbing hers in the nick of time, holding her steady.

"You all right?" he whispered.

"Yes." Her voice cracked as she realized how close she'd come to falling the rest of the way down the trail. Ryker's hand was strong, but not painfully so and she gripped it like the lifeline it was. "Thanks."

"We have to keep going." His low voice held an unmistakable urgency. She nodded and continued down the path, doing her best to keep from slipping on another rock.

"I thought we were playing hide-and-seek?" Aaron's tone was plaintive.

"We are," Ryker assured him. "Shh."

Thankfully, Aaron stuck his thumb in his mouth.

Their progress seemed incredibly slow and she knew that it was her fault. But even though she felt Ryker's tall, lean frame behind her, she never once heard him sigh impatiently, the way she knew Tim would have.

Enough. She couldn't keep comparing Ryker to Tim in her mind. Her husband was gone, had frankly disappeared emotionally long before he'd died.

She needed to stay strong and focused on surviving, for Aaron's sake and for the baby.

When she stumbled across a fork in the trail, she paused and glanced over her shoulder at Ryker. "Which way?"

"Right."

Right? That path went uphill, while the other one led down. Her instincts were to keep going down, but she didn't question Ryker's decision.

If she thought heading down was difficult because she couldn't see her feet, climbing up was even worse. Sure, she could see the trail ahead of her as they went, but it didn't take long for her to begin panting heavily with exertion.

At this rate, the bad guys would find them within seconds by following the sound of her breathing louder than a wounded buffalo.

Her thigh muscles were on fire and it was all she could do to keep from groaning out loud as she forced herself to keep climbing. Praying helped for a while, but then even that was too much work. When she stopped, even for a moment, she felt Ryker's hand on her lower back, keeping her steady without pressuring her to go faster.

She kept climbing, for him. For Aaron. For the baby.

I can do this.

The words became a chant in her mind, until she couldn't think of anything other than taking the next step, then the next. *I can do this.* Sweat slid down the sides of her face, dampening her hair and her clothes.

Still, she climbed.

The only good thing about heading up was that they were getting closer to the woods. Tall trees full of leaves rustled overhead, providing desperately needed shade from the hot morning sun.

When she thought she couldn't take another

step, she felt Ryker's hand on her shoulder. "See the rock over there? We'll stop there for now."

She wanted to sink instantly to the ground but managed to find the strength to take the necessary steps toward the large boulder protruding from the mountain.

"Sit here, beneath the edge of the rock." Ryker's whisper along with the fact that he wanted her to hide beneath the boulder indicated they weren't safe yet.

Gratefully, she sat down and scooted as far under the outcropping as possible. Then she lifted her hands for Aaron.

"I don't wanna play hide-and-seek anymore," he complained. "I'm hungry."

Ryker set her bag beside her. "I need you to stay here. I'll be back soon."

Despite her bone-weary exhaustion, she lunged for his hand. "Don't leave us."

He knelt so he was eye level with her, his thumb lightly caressing the back of her hand. "I won't be long. I need to get up higher, to see the trail."

She knew he meant he needed to see the men who were desperate to find them.

To find *her*.

Clutching Aaron close, she tried to keep from falling apart. "Okay," she whispered. "We'll be fine."

Ryker nodded and released her, rising to his feet. He moved silently away, leaving her and Aaron alone beneath the rock, surrounded by woods.

Closing her eyes, she noiselessly prayed the way Willa had taught her.

Dear Lord, please give Ryker the strength he needs to keep us all safe. Watch over us and guide us on Your chosen path. Amen.

Her eyes pricked with tears when she thought about Willa. The woman had willingly opened her heart and her home to a pregnant stranger, and Liv knew she'd be forever thankful for the way Willa had brought her into the church and shown her the way to God.

Why had the kind woman died? Was that really part of God's plan? She sniffled and tried to brush away her tears. This wasn't the time to wallow in pity. Willa would want her to be strong for Aaron and her unborn child.

"I'm hungry," Aaron said again, making her realize she'd forgotten.

"I have your breakfast bagel." She rummaged in the bag, finding the slightly squished sandwich. After opening it for Aaron, she gave it to him. The egg and cheese were more than a little melted, but he ate with gusto.

Knowing she needed to keep up her own strength, she unwrapped her sandwich and forced herself to take a bite. She wasn't hungry, but could feel the baby kicking and knew they both needed fuel if she were to keep going.

The idea of climbing the mountain again made her swallow a moan. She wasn't sure her legs would last for much longer. Even at rest, her thigh muscles were quivering. Not only was she carrying the extra weight of her pregnancy, but she'd never been one of those women who worked out in the gym. She'd always preferred long walks to running or lifting weights.

But now she realized just how out of shape she really was. And that her lack of physical endurance could easily get them all killed.

Silently promising to join a gym once the baby was born, she finished her sandwich. Aaron finished his, too, and then began to squirm in her lap.

"I wanna walk." He leaned forward, in an attempt to crawl off her lap.

"Shh." She squelched a surge of panic that Aaron might throw a temper tantrum that would lead the bad guys straight to them. "We're still playing hide-and-seek. We're hiding beneath the rock so that no one will find us."

For a moment, he seemed agreeable to continue the game. Aaron crawled off her lap and went farther beneath the rock. She didn't stop him, hoping that allowing him some ability to move around would help keep him quiet.

A pair of black-denim-clad legs abruptly dropped down on the ground in front of her. She almost screamed, until she recognized Ryker.

She put a hand over her racing heart, swallowing the urge to snap at him. He'd been so quiet, she hadn't heard him approach. "You scared me," she accused in a harsh whisper.

"Sorry." His hazel eyes looked at her for a long moment, and she put a hand to her disheveled hair, wishing she didn't look like a sweaty whale. "I want you to take my phone."

Confused, she looked from the cell phone in his hand back to him. "Why?"

He hesitated. "I called a couple of friends for help. I'm hoping they'll call back soon. The phone is on vibrate, so it won't ring."

"Friends?" Warily, she took the phone, the device warm from his touch. "Are you sure we can trust them?"

"With my life."

And mine? The words hovered on her lips, but she managed to hold them back. Ryker had protected her and Aaron over and over again. There was no reason to doubt his loyalty now. "Okay."

He nodded. "They're in Milwaukee, so it will take them at least eight to nine hours to get here by car."

Eight to nine hours? The spark of hope in her chest withered and died. "That's a long time."

"I know." The corner of his mouth quirked in a smile. "I'm planning to meet them halfway."

"How?"

"Trust me, okay?" She wanted to ask more, but Ryker rose to his feet. "I'll be back as soon as possible."

With that, he was gone, melting into the brush as silently as he'd arrived. It occurred to her that he must have been an incredible soldier.

She picked up the phone and stared at the screen, willing it to flash with an incoming call.

Friends of Ryker helping them would certainly level the playing field, yet she couldn't help feeling a bit guilty.

Ryker and now his friends were putting their lives on the line for her and Aaron. It was noble of them to protect her like this.

And for the moment, all she could do in return was pray.

After placing a call to both Duncan O'Hare and Mike Callahan and giving the phone to Olivia, Ryker returned to his hiding spot at the top of the hill. He watched the two men dressed in black, carrying small handguns, as they made their way down the trail. It hadn't taken them long to figure out where he and Olivia had gone.

When they'd paused at the fork, he'd held his breath, as they exchanged a short, terse discussion.

As he'd hoped, they'd split up. The taller of the two headed down the path, the shorter guy nimbly climbing up the way he and Olivia had.

That meant he only had one to deal with for now, although he suspected it wouldn't be long before the taller guy realized he'd been duped and joined the shorter man who was now hot on their trail.

With all the patience and skill embedded in him from his time in Afghanistan, Ryker watched the shorter of the two mercenaries cautiously approach. He could tell, even from this distance, the guy was nervous.

Ryker knew the guy he'd knocked out must have managed to see them getting into his SUV and leaving town to have found them so quickly. This time, he needed to make sure he did something more to ensure them a getaway.

There were moments when he lost sight of the approaching mercenary, but waited without moving for him to reappear in his line of vision.

As the guy approached the landing point Ryker had identified as the target spot, he readied himself. Three. Two. One. Without a sound, Ryker launched himself off the hill, landing on top of the mercenary with a loud thud.

They rolled together, precariously close to the edge, with Ryker managing to come out on top. He pressed against the guy's carotid arteries until he passed out, then quickly used the plastic zip ties he always carried in his pockets to bind the man's wrists and ankles.

Once he had the mercenary trussed up like a Thanksgiving turkey, he dragged him off the trail, deep into the brush. The whole takedown had gone off without either man saying a word.

For a moment, Ryker peered into the man's face, trying to remember if he'd seen him before, in those days before Christmas when he'd helped Hawk and his family escape from similar mercenaries sent by the Blake-Moore Group.

But the guy was a stranger.

For a moment he sat back on his heels, trying to understand how the Blake-Moore Group had managed to recruit more soldiers. The entire operation should have been broken up by the capture and imprisonment of Todd Hayes from the Department of Defense.

Ryker went through the guy's pockets searching for an ID but found nothing other than a password protected phone, which he tossed into the ravine. More proof, at least in his mind, that the two men were sent from the Blake-Moore Group. When he had the guy well hidden, Ryker took his weapon, tucked it into the waistband at the small of his back, then stood.

One down, one more to go.

He made his way back up to the hilltop. He wanted to go back to the large boulder where Olivia and Aaron waited, to check on them and reassure them, but he needed to keep his eye on the trail below.

There was no telling how long he'd have to wait before the second mercenary showed up. He was a patient man by nature, but couldn't help being concerned over Olivia and Aaron.

As if on cue, he heard Aaron telling his mother he was tired of playing hide-and-seek and wanted to go home. She reassured him that they'd be leaving soon, but Aaron wasn't buying it. Their voices weren't too loud; he was listening intently, which was why he'd heard them, yet he couldn't deny the sound could carry all the way down to where the second guy was lurking on the trail.

Once he might have prayed for strength, but that was before he'd lost his girlfriend and her daughter. Before his entire world had turned upside down. Right now, all he did was try to ignore their voices.

Just a little longer, he hoped.

Finally, after what seemed like forever, he heard the sound of heavy footsteps on the trail.

Thankfully, he no longer heard Olivia and Aaron. The taller guy wasn't as stealthy as the first was, maybe because he was growing tired of chasing shadows through the woods.

A fact that would work in Ryker's favor.

"Steve? Where are you?" The mercenary's voice was full of annoyance and the fact that he'd called out to his buddy made Ryker smile.

Steve, huh? These guys wouldn't have lasted long in Afghanistan. It seemed the caliber of the soldiers the Blake-Moore Group recruited had gone downhill.

As before, he waited with infinite patience for the mercenary to get into position. As the guy approached, he slowed his pace, as if sensing danger. Ryker gave him points for realizing something wasn't right.

Just a few feet more…

Now! For the second time that day, Ryker launched himself from his hiding spot. Unfortunately, at the last second, the mercenary turned and lifted his hands in a defensive move as Ryker landed on him. They rolled over and over, Ryker's head hitting a rock and sending shards of pain lancing through him.

Darkness threatened, but he refused to give up. He tightened his grip and fought with every ounce of strength he possessed, finally gaining the upper hand.

The mercenary grunted and let out a harsh expletive. Ryker pressed harder on the guy's neck, willing him to surrender to unconsciousness.

A minute later, the mercenary went slack. Still, he didn't release the pressure, fearing a trap.

Finally, he eased up and hung his head for a moment. The base of his skull throbbed, but he ignored it. Once again, he reached for the plastic zip ties, and bound the second guy's wrists and ankles.

"Ryker? Are you okay?"

Olivia's voice had him spinning around so fast, the landscape dipped and shimmered. He blinked, bringing her into focus. "Fine." His tone was sharper than he'd intended, but the thought of her watching him struggle to subdue the mercenary bothered him. "Go back to the rock. I'll be there shortly."

Her gaze clung to his for a moment, before she eased backward, out of sight. He wanted to close his eyes, make the pain in his head and his thigh go away, but he needed to finish this.

After dragging the second perp to where he'd stashed the first one, he debated whether or not to wait for them to regain consciousness. He wanted to interrogate the two men, to find out who they worked for and what they wanted from Olivia. At the same time, though, he desperately needed to get her and Aaron far away from there.

Logically, he knew that sticking around to question the men would be useless. Even if he managed to get them to talk, he doubted the men would tell him anything truthful.

He took a moment to zip-tie the two men together, and to a tree, so they couldn't get too far once they awoke. He tossed the second guy's phone into the ravine as well, then tore their T-shirts into strips to use as gags, to keep them silent. He figured the two guys would be found eventually, by other hikers or tourists, but hoped to gain enough of a head start that it wouldn't matter.

Killing them would give him and Olivia more time to escape, but he couldn't do it. No way could he outright kill a man, even a gun-wielding jerk who'd come after him, not to mention a pregnant woman and a child.

He'd seen too much death while he was in Afghanistan, and here at home.

When he'd learned of his girlfriend's and her daughter's deaths, he'd promised himself he'd only take a life in self-defense. The way he had at the nanny's house. It had been necessary to shoot the man who had Aaron, in order to save the boy's life.

Still, he hesitated. Their escape from the Shawnee National Forest wouldn't be fast, especially since Olivia couldn't exactly run back down the mountain, then back up again, the way they'd come. The last thing he needed was to send her into premature labor.

Finally, he turned away. He could only hope that Duncan and Mike would be on their way soon.

At this point, Ryker would take all the help he could get.

FIVE

In Liv's opinion, the trek back down the mountain, then up again was more difficult than before. Maybe because the rush of adrenaline had faded, leaving a shaky exhaustion in its wake.

Her leg muscles ached, but she knew that Ryker likely felt worse. Watching him wrestle with the mercenary on the ground had been a harsh reminder of the magnitude of danger.

She was blessed to have Ryker as their protector.

Biting back another moan, she pushed onward. The danger had been mitigated for the moment, but she knew that this was only a temporary reprieve.

The Blake-Moore Group wouldn't stop until they got whatever they wanted.

She just wished she knew exactly what that was.

As she crested the hill, the fast-food restaurant was a welcome sight. She wanted nothing more than to go inside to cool off, but Ryker steered her around to the front of the building.

"We'll get something for you and Aaron soon." His deep, rumbly voice was close to her ear. "Right now we need to get out of here."

She nodded, understanding he was right. The more distance they put between them and the two men from the Blake-Moore Group, the better.

But he surprised her by pulling open the back door of his SUV and gesturing to the car seat. "Pull that out of there, would you?"

Confused, she glanced up at him. "Why? Don't we need it?"

"Yes, but we're taking their SUV instead of this one."

"Oh." Understanding dawned. Since he was still holding Aaron and her diaper bag, she did as he'd asked, pulling the car seat out of the back and carrying it over to the black SUV at the end of the row.

After buckling in the seat, she stepped back so Ryker could strap Aaron inside. Then he leaned over and dropped the zebra bag on the floor of the front passenger seat.

Sliding into the mercenary's vehicle gave her the creeps, but she shook off the sensation. Who was she to argue with Ryker's plan? All she wanted was for her and Aaron to be safe.

She rubbed a hand over her belly.

"Are you okay?" Ryker's voice held a note of concern.

"Fine." She managed a weak smile. "Just tired. That's the most exercise I've had in a very long time."

"I'm sorry." A deep frown furrowed Ryker's forehead. "It was the best option we had to get away."

"I know." And his plan had worked. She rested her head back against the seat and momentarily closed her eyes.

"I'll stop soon for water, okay?"

She opened her eyes and looked over at him. Ryker was still frowning as if he'd done something wrong. "Thank you."

His jaw tightened. "For nearly getting you and Aaron hurt or worse?"

"For saving our lives. Again." She didn't like the self-recrimination in his tone, so she reached out and lightly touched his forearm. His skin was warm, and she ignored the shimmer of awareness. "We wouldn't be alive without you. I'm not sure why you came after me and Aaron, but I believe God sent you to save us."

He looked surprised. "I run my own security consulting business, so safety is always my top priority."

"I see." She was glad that he was so good at

his job. She stared out the windshield. It took a moment for her to realize they were heading north, back toward Wisconsin, where this mess had started.

She swallowed a protest and dropped her hand into her lap. Ryker had mentioned contacting two friends to help them, so she wasn't going to complain.

Even if her original plan was to never set foot in the state of Wisconsin ever again.

"I'm just glad I found you." His voice was low and gravelly, and she wondered if he wasn't a believer. Which was a shame, because he was one of the most honorable men she'd ever met.

"Me, too." She remembered how suspicious she'd been about his motives for helping her. Foolish now, when he'd done nothing but save them over and over again. "Although I'd still like to know why you decided to track me down in the first place."

He hesitated before answering. "I told you, I was at your house and noticed that you and Aaron had left in a hurry. I was concerned about your safety, especially since I knew your husband and brother were…"

Dead. He hadn't said the word, but she knew what he'd meant.

Dropping the issue seemed to be the prudent thing to do.

"Oh!" She rummaged in her zebra bag. "I almost forgot. I'm sure it's cold, but here's your breakfast sandwich."

"Thanks." He ate while he drove, downing the food in less than five bites. She was sure he was still hungry, but didn't think he'd appreciate the animal crackers she carried for Aaron.

They'd need to stop for food and fuel, sooner than later. She'd returned his phone, upset that neither of his friends had returned his call, and now wondered about that. "Would you like me to try contacting your friends again?"

Ryker pulled his phone out of his pocket and tossed it into her lap. "Why not? They're both cops, so it could be that they're at work and can't talk. We may not hear from them until their respective shifts are over."

They were both cops? She shivered, despite the June sun beating in through the windows. She turned the phone in her fingers. "I...don't trust cops."

He raised a brow. "They're my friends. They would never do anything to hurt you, the baby or Aaron. Mike is married to Duncan's sister Shayla, and they have a child of their own, a boy named Brodie who is just a little older than Aaron. I've helped them out before, and I know they're more than willing to return the favor."

She swallowed a lump of fear and tried to be

rational. "I...didn't know you had friends in law enforcement."

"I would trust both of them with my life. Yours and Aaron's, too." Ryker's tone was soft. "They're good guys. And they've worked outside the lines on more than one occasion."

Worked outside the lines? Meaning, not following the rules to the strictest level of the law? Knowing that should have made her feel better, but didn't.

"Okay." She tried to inject confidence in her tone. "I hope you're right."

"I promise—it will be okay."

She made the calls, but was forced to leave messages for both men. "Still no answer."

"They'll call as soon as they're able." He paused, then added, "I know I've asked you this before, but there has to be a good reason why these guys are coming after you."

"I've been racking my brain trying to understand that myself. I mean, sure, I overheard a few things, here and there, but nothing serious enough to make them come after me."

"Like what?" There was a note of urgency in his tone.

She watched as he pulled into a drive-through fast-food restaurant and ordered several bottles of water. "Get yourself something more to eat," she encouraged.

"I'm fine." He handed her a cold bottle of water and she gratefully took a long drink. The nagging headache that she sometimes experienced when dehydrated eased off a notch.

"I heard Colin and Tim saying something about selling weapons to the enemy." It wasn't easy to discuss how her husband and brother had betrayed their country. "At the time I wasn't sure what that meant, but I soon figured out something was off when I was locked in the motel room with Jeff."

"There was no way for you to know the details," Ryker assured her. "What else?"

She thought back. The snippets of conversation were often out of context and hadn't made any sense. "Something about a stash of money, but that was likely referring to the gun sales."

"Probably." Ryker kept a keen eye on the rearview mirror in a way that convinced her they weren't safe yet. "Anything else?"

"Not really." She sighed and rubbed her stomach again. It was something she did unconsciously, to soothe both herself and the baby. "I did get the sense they were trying to keep secrets from their boss."

There was a moment of silence as Ryker digested that bit of information.

When his phone rang, it startled them both. He gestured for her to answer it.

The name on the screen was Duncan O'Hare. "Hello?"

"Is this Olivia Habush?"

"Yes. I'm here with Ryker. Let me put you on speaker." She held the phone in the palm of her hand and used the speaker function for Ryker's sake.

"I hear you're in trouble." Duncan's voice was matter-of-fact.

"I need help. We're just leaving the Shawnee National Forest, heading north through Illinois toward Wisconsin. I was hoping you and Mike could hit the road and meet us halfway."

"I'm happy to meet up with you. I just have to find someone to cover my next couple of shifts."

"Great." Ryker sounded relieved. "I'm avoiding Interstate 57, using highway 51 instead. I was hoping you guys could meet us either in Springfield or Bloomington, depending on when you can get moving."

"I'll see what I can do, and get in touch with Mike, too." There was a pause before Duncan added, "I assume you need the usual?"

"Yes, please." Ryker smiled, and Liv realized it was probably the first time she'd seen him smile since they'd met. Had it really been only yesterday? He was even better looking when he smiled. "Appreciate it."

"Okay. Give me some time to coordinate with Mike. I'll let you know when we're on our way."

"Thanks, Duncan. Appreciate your help."

"Hey, it's the least I can do. You guys left me out of the fun when Hawk needed help, so it's my turn."

Ryker's smile widened. "Later."

Duncan disconnected the line, so she pushed the End Call button. "Left him out of the fun when Hawk needed help? I hardly view dealing with the Blake-Moore Group as *fun*."

Ryker shrugged. "That's just his way of keeping things light. Cops, like soldiers, put their lives on the line every single day. If they didn't make jokes, they wouldn't be able to do their jobs."

He had a point. "I guess."

"Duncan served with me and Hawk over in Afghanistan." Ryker glanced at her, his gaze serious. "He knew your brother and husband."

The news was sobering. She stared down at her hands resting on her belly. The indentation around the fourth finger of her left hand wasn't noticeable anymore, likely because she was retaining a bit of water weight. Still, she couldn't help rubbing the spot where her wedding ring had once rested.

She and Tim had exchanged vows to love and

cherish one another, but she eventually realized their marriage was a farce.

Ignoring the signs of their marriage unraveling had been stupid. Learning about God and faith these past two months had made her error in judgment glaringly obvious.

It was a mistake she wouldn't make again. Marriage wasn't something to take lightly, and she knew that from this point on, she was better off alone.

The way Olivia was rubbing the fourth finger of her left hand bothered him. Was she grappling with the fact that he'd been a part of the team who'd killed her brother and husband? He couldn't blame her, yet if she'd known how her brother had pointed a gun at four-year-old Lizzie, she'd be horrified.

Not his place to tell her.

He decided to focus on the fact that Duncan and hopefully Mike were on the way, with new disposable phones, a new SUV and enough cash that they could stay off-grid for a long time. He didn't want anything that might leave a trail back to him.

It had been a gamble to take the Blake-Moore SUV. Most of the new models had built-in GPS devices, and once the two gunmen he'd tied up managed to get free, they'd be intent on tracking the vehicle. But they'd need to hot-wire his SUV or get another first. Time that would work in their favor.

He'd have to ditch their vehicle soon. He'd brought several thousand in cash with him, but his reserves would take a hit when he purchased a replacement car.

But it was worth it, to keep the three lives in his care safe from harm.

His headache had faded to a dull throb. He'd taken some over-the-counter medication when they'd stopped at the gas station. Then he'd cleaned up the blood from the back of his head the best he could, without mentioning the wound to Olivia. She didn't need anything more to worry about.

He was worrying enough for both of them.

"I meant to ask earlier, do you know Tim's cousin, too?"

Cousin? He turned to look at her. This was the first he'd heard of a cousin. "Maybe. What's the name?"

"Seth Willis. He served overseas with Tim and Colin, too." She frowned. "Although, now that I think about it, I don't know that they were in the same unit."

He searched his memory but came up empty. "I can't say the name rings a bell. Did Seth also join the Blake-Moore Group?"

She bit her lip, her brow wrinkling as she considered his question. "I think so. I think he might have been at the first cookout that the guys had when they initially joined the group."

"Good to know." It was a great clue to follow up on. Was it possible the cousin was out to vindicate the deaths of Tim and Colin?

No, that wasn't logical, either. Olivia and Aaron were innocent bystanders in all of this. There would be no reason on earth for Willis to come after her with armed men.

It had to be one of the two founders of the organization, either Kevin Blake or Harper Moore, or both, who had sent the mercenaries after Olivia.

Nothing else made sense.

"Um, Ryker?"

He glanced at Olivia. "What?"

"I need to go to the bathroom." Her cheeks were pink as if she was embarrassed to mention it. "And it would be good for Aaron to go, too."

"Oh sure. Of course." He mentally berated himself for not thinking of that sooner. He hadn't been around when his girlfriend was pregnant; he'd met her a year or so after she'd given birth to her daughter. But it made sense that frequent trips to the bathroom were symptoms expectant mothers dealt with.

"I think there's a gas station up ahead." She avoided his gaze, still rubbing her belly.

"Works for me." He eyed the gas gauge, deciding they were fine for now.

He wasn't inclined to leave a full tank of gas for when the mercenaries eventually found the SUV. In fact, he'd prefer to leave the tank dry as a bone.

The stop at the gas station took longer than he liked. It seemed like Olivia and Aaron were in the bathroom for a long time, then they went through the small convenience store, picking out snacks.

When Olivia reached inside her oversize bag, he stopped her with a hand on her arm. "I've got it."

"It's fine. I have money."

He ignored her protest and paid for the items in cash. When he noticed she'd included a couple of toys for Aaron, he realized that was yet another thing he should have thought about while he'd been watching over them.

To be fair, the little boy had been great while they'd hidden on the mountain. He'd expected a lot of crying or complaining. But Aaron had been remarkably well behaved.

When everyone was settled in the SUV, he hit the road again, keeping an eye on his rearview mirror. So far, there had been no sign of the mercenaries, but he knew it was only a matter of time.

Fifteen minutes later, he noticed a sign advertising a used-car lot. When they approached, he pulled off the highway and headed toward it.

"What are you doing?" Olivia's voice reflected her concern.

"We need a new set of wheels." He offered a smile. "Don't worry—this won't take long."

"But…" She rubbed her hands over her stomach, a gesture he'd noticed she used when she was upset. "I thought we'd use this car until we met up with Mike and Duncan."

"These SUVs have GPS devices built into them. The sooner we ditch it, the better."

"You mean, they could use the GPS device to find us?" Her voice squeaked in protest.

"Yes, but I have a plan." He pulled into the lot and threw the gearshift into Park. "Let's go."

Her blue eyes darkened with apprehension, but she unbuckled her seat belt and slid out of the car. She grabbed the diaper bag, leaving him to get Aaron out of his car seat.

"I'll take that." He didn't want her carrying anything heavy. He glanced around at the options available to them. "Look for something under five thousand dollars. It only has to get us to Springfield or Bloomington, so nothing fancy."

She nodded, and began peering at the stickers on the vehicles closest to them. It didn't take long for a salesman, likely the owner, to come out to meet them.

"What can I help you folks with today?"

"We're looking for a car." Ryker knew the guy was just trying to be cordial, since there was no other reason for them to stop in a used-car lot. "Something with a reliable engine, yet not too expensive."

"How about this one?" Olivia stood beside a dark blue sedan with several spots of rust.

"I have a van over here." The salesman gestured to a large Dodge Caravan. If he thought it was odd that they'd arrived in a new SUV, he didn't let on. "Perfect for a growing family."

"Maybe give us a few minutes alone." He smiled to take the sting from his tone.

"Sure, sure." The guy pulled out a business card. "Name's Bill Sommers. Let me know when you're ready."

With Bill out of the way, he made his way down the row of cars. They were more expensive than he'd planned, the dark blue one coming in at exactly five thousand.

Then he found a tan sedan with a decent price. "What do you think?" He looked at Olivia.

"Looks good. I say we take it."

Before he could call out to Bill, the salesman came rushing over. "Find something you like?"

"We'll take this one. Will you give me a deal to pay in cash?"

"Cash?" Bill's eyes practically popped out of his head. "Sure. How about five hundred off the price?"

"Sold." Ryker managed to keep smiling, but felt edgy. He wanted to pay the man and get out of there, pronto.

They followed Bill inside. Ten minutes later, they had the keys in hand.

"I'll just get the car seat." Olivia hurried over to the black SUV.

"Uh, you're not leaving that here, are you?" For the first time since their arrival, Bill looked concerned.

"Don't worry, a couple of friends will be by to pick it up, although I'd appreciate it if you would shred my personal information while I watch. I'm careful that way."

"I guess." The guy shrugged and did as Ryker asked.

Ryker smiled in satisfaction and shook Bill's hand. "Thanks again."

As they drove out of the parking lot in the tan sedan, he thought he caught a glimpse of a familiar black SUV several miles behind them. The flat terrain made it easy to watch their six.

He tightened his grip on the wheel and did his best not to panic.

There were lots of black SUVs on the road, he told himself. It was a popular color. They were safe, for now.

He sped up, putting more distance between them. Maybe it was time to try the interstate, where the speed limit was higher.

As he approached an entrance ramp, he noticed the black SUV wasn't on the road anymore.

Because the mercenaries had turned into the used-car lot?

If so, it wouldn't take long for the two men to get back on the trail. Despite his warning, he figured Bill would blab all about the vehicle they'd just purchased for cash.

Ryker knew they needed to get to Duncan and Mike as soon as humanly possible.

Before the mercenaries caught up to them.

SIX

Something was wrong. The way Ryker kept staring up at the rearview mirror was concerning.

"What is it? Have they found us?" She twisted in her seat, no easy feat with her belly, to glance behind them. There were plenty of cars on the interstate, but nothing that seemed out of the ordinary.

Not that she was an expert.

"We'll be fine." Ryker's calm voice didn't quite match the dark shadow in his hazel eyes. "We'll have help from Duncan and Mike soon."

"I know." She told herself that Ryker had already gotten her and Aaron safely out of harm's way several times already. No reason to think he couldn't do it again, if needed. Besides, they were in a different car now, a tactic that should help them escape the men from the Blake-Moore Group. Although she still didn't understand why they were after her.

Smoothing her hand over her belly, she tried to remain calm. Stress wasn't good for her or the baby.

She was glad to know she had six weeks left before her due date. Surely all this running would be over before then.

Wouldn't it?

"Whee, I'm flying." Aaron held the toy plane in his chubby fist and waved it around in the air, making dips and turns. "Mommy, I wanna be a pilot someday."

"I'm sure you will."

"He's a great kid." Ryker's voice was low. "I'm amazed he's holding up so well."

"Me, too." She glanced back at her son, who was content to play by himself for a while. The cheap toys she'd purchased at the gas station were a welcome diversion. "He hasn't asked for his father in months." The statement popped out before she could stop it.

"He hasn't?" Ryker threw her a sidelong glance.

She slowly shook her head and stared blindly out the windshield for a bit. "Tim wasn't around much, even before…" Her voice trailed off.

Before he was killed.

"I'm sorry." She wasn't sure if Ryker's apology was for her loss, or for the role he'd played in her husband's death.

She shook off the dark thoughts. "It's okay. I'm just glad Aaron isn't missing him too badly."

Ryker nodded but didn't say anything else. She wondered about his past personal relationships. He didn't wear a wedding ring and never indicated he was married, but for all she knew, he had a woman waiting for him back home—wherever that was.

Not that Ryker's personal life was any of her business.

Except hadn't he said something about tracking her for the past few weeks? Did that mean his girlfriend didn't mind him being gone for long periods of time?

If the situation was reversed, she'd mind.

She cast another glance at him, subtly studying his profile. His dark hair was short, his cheekbones prominent. There was a dark stubble shadowing his cheeks, which normally wasn't her thing, but now made him look even more attractive in a rugged sort of way. His strong muscles beneath his black T-shirt were not bad on the eyes, either.

Enough. She peeled her gaze away to stare out the windshield. They were running for their lives from armed men. Why was she noticing Ryker's looks? Must be that her hormones were all out of whack.

Yep, that was it. Hormones.

She didn't want a man in her life. Honestly, all she wanted was to be safe. To raise her son. To bring her baby into the world.

And a place to call home.

Tears pricked her eyes, and she quickly brushed them away. There wasn't time for a pity party. Hadn't she learned from church services that God was always with her? Always watching over her? She often felt His presence when she prayed.

Between God and Ryker, she and Aaron and the baby were safe.

And that was all that mattered.

Exhaustion swept over her. She closed her eyes and rested her head against the window.

The baby moved and kicked, making her smile. She placed her hand over the motion, wishing she dared share the moment with Ryker.

"Active today?" Ryker's dry comment made her realize his keen gaze missed nothing.

"Apparently only when I want to rest." She wryly shook her head. "Happens all the time."

Ryker's gaze landed briefly on her belly, then shifted quickly back to the road. Before she could say anything more, his phone rang.

She picked it up from the center console, then pressed the Talk and Speaker buttons. "Hello?"

"Olivia?"

"Yes." She glanced at Ryker. "Duncan, is that you?"

"Yeah, I assume Ryker is there listening in?"

"I'm here," Ryker said.

"Well, I've got good news and bad." Despite the former, Duncan's tone held regret. "The good news is that I have Mike following me in his own SUV, so we can give you guys one to use. The bad news is that we're running late. We weren't planning on a semitruck colliding into a pickup. As if the stupid toll roads and Chicago traffic didn't slow us down enough."

"Yeah, I hear you on the tolls. We're about two hours out of Bloomington. We'll still plan to meet there. When we arrive, I'll let you know which motel we're at."

"Sounds like a plan. Later." Duncan disconnected from the call.

She dropped Ryker's phone back in the pocket of the console. "I hate to tell you, but I'll need another bathroom break in the not-too-distant future."

If he thought she was annoying, he didn't let on. "Can you make it another ten miles to the rest stop?"

"Sure." She winced when the baby kicked her bladder. This pregnancy felt very different from her first and she couldn't help wondering if the difference was just the fact she was completely on her own, or if this baby might be a girl.

Honestly, the gender didn't matter to her, as long as the baby was healthy.

No premature labor allowed.

Ryker pulled off at the rest stop. Hopefully this would be the last time they'd need to take a break before reaching their destination. She unbuckled her seat belt and levered herself out of the car, her thigh muscles groaning in protest after the morning climb.

Ryker pulled Aaron out of his car seat, then swung her zebra bag over his shoulder. Oddly, she found the way he carried the diaper bag endearing.

"Let Aaron walk," she suggested. "He needs to burn off some energy."

Ryker put the boy down and he immediately started to run toward the building. Liv hurried after her son.

The bathroom break lasted longer than it should have, but considering how good Aaron had been, she couldn't make herself cut his playtime short. To his credit Ryker didn't say a word, although she could sense his impatience to hit the road.

Unlike her husband, whose temper had been razor sharp and quickly triggered the last few weeks of their marriage.

"Thanks," she said, when they were finally

back on the interstate. "I know that waiting around made you crazy."

He shrugged. "Not really. The extra time was helpful in making sure no one followed us. So far, so good."

Her smile dimmed. "I'm glad."

Ryker's intuition, the way he stayed alert at all times, was instinctive for him. He didn't even have to think about what to do. And he never complained.

She couldn't imagine living like that, constantly watching your back.

This was clearly his world. One she didn't particularly care for.

Once the danger was over, she knew Ryker would move on to something else. And that was a good thing.

She wanted nothing more than to find another accounting job and settle down in a quiet place to take care of her new baby and her son. And while she'd miss the calming, supportive side of Ryker's nature, she knew their worlds would never mesh.

It was foolish to wish for something more between them.

Ryker's gut was twisted in knots, although he did his best to hide the tension. The last thing he needed was for Olivia to pick up on his concern.

He desperately wanted to meet up with Duncan and Mike. The two men flanking his six would make him feel much better. While Aaron had run around chasing butterflies, he'd secretly watched the highway, trying to decide which of the black SUVs that went past might be the mercenaries.

The vehicles whizzed past without slowing, so he felt certain they were safe.

But ditching the tan sedan was still a top priority.

The vehicle ran well enough, eating the miles to Bloomington, with flat, boring countryside whizzing past them. He preferred woods or mountains that were nice to look at while providing cover, but the lack of cover went both ways.

And hopefully they'd be back in Wisconsin in the next day or so.

He passed the first few Bloomington exits, searching for something a bit more remote. Maybe the north side of town, where they'd be just a little closer to their ultimate destination.

Olivia shifted in her seat, and he knew she was uncomfortable sitting for so long.

"Almost there," he assured her.

"There, where?" The smile that curved her lips made his breath catch in his throat. She was stunning when she smiled, and he told himself he was a jerk for even thinking of her as an attractive woman.

Not only was she pregnant but he'd helped kill her brother and the father of her children. The fact that she didn't seem to blame him was humbling. Still, he knew more of the grim details than she did. "Keep your eyes peeled for something farther off the interstate. Something that won't be easy to target."

"Not easy to target." She paled and he inwardly smacked himself for using such a blunt term. "Okay, then."

"Use my phone to find something small and outside the city proper."

"I found a motel that advertises two-bedroom suites for a decent price," she said to him a few minutes later. "Take the second exit."

He did and found the place. It wasn't a highly rated motel, but it would work. After pulling up near the lobby, he took his phone and called Duncan to let him know where they were.

"Got it. We're finally past the accident scene, so we should make good time from here."

"Great." He couldn't hide the relief. Soon he'd have more than enough backup. "See you soon."

He booked a suite on the first floor for easy access. He paid in cash, but was forced to use a credit card for incidental expenses. He convinced the manager not to run the card until they checked out by giving him another fifty bucks.

The suite was a bit musty, but overall clean. He carried the car seat and Olivia's bag in and set them near the doorway. Aaron was thrilled to be out of his car seat, running around the room with his new toys. Olivia stretched out on top of the bed with a low groan.

"Where are my ankles?" She looked down toward her elevated feet with a forlorn expression. "I had them a month ago, but now they've disappeared."

He wasn't sure how to respond, so he changed the subject. "Are you hungry? I can grab us something to eat while we wait for the guys to arrive."

"I'm always hungry, but it feels like we should wait for the guys."

"They won't mind. There's a fast-food restaurant across the street. I'll pick up something to go."

She didn't look thrilled, but pushed herself upright. "Okay."

He didn't want to leave her alone, but he could see how tired she was. "You look exhausted. Why don't you rest for a bit? Just tell me what you'd like, and I'll head over with Aaron."

She hesitated, uncertainty shadowing her gaze. Finally, she nodded. "Thanks. I'll have a grilled-chicken sandwich if they have it. Otherwise a cheeseburger."

"Grilled chicken." He nodded and held out his hand toward Aaron. "Ready to take a walk?"

For the first time, the child hung back, as if he wasn't sure about leaving with a stranger. Ryker was glad the boy was wary, but didn't like the idea of scaring him.

"Go on, Aaron," Liv encouraged. "I'll be here when you get back."

"All right. But can I get a toy?"

"Sure." He felt certain there would be a toy in the kid's meal.

Aaron crossed over and put his small hand in Ryker's. The trust in Aaron's gaze was nearly his undoing. He couldn't stand the idea of the little boy and his pregnant mother being in danger.

They needed to track down the men in charge of the Blake-Moore Group, and soon.

Outside, the warm early June sun was still high in the sky. He swept his gaze around the motel parking lot before heading out toward the restaurant.

He didn't think they'd been followed, but couldn't shake the impending sense of doom. Maybe once Duncan and Mike arrived, he'd be able to relax a bit.

The line was long at the height of the dinner hour. While he and Aaron waited, the kid changed his mind several times before settling on chicken strips.

When he had their meals and more bottles of water securely tucked into the to-go bags, he took Aaron's hand again and walked him back over to the motel. Still nothing appeared out of place, but he hoped Duncan and Mike would get there soon.

He entered the suite and tiptoed across the main living area to the bedroom where Olivia had been resting. She was asleep. The peaceful expression on her face was like a sucker punch to the gut.

She deserved to look that restful every day. Not chased by jerks with guns.

"Mommy?"

"Shh." He put a finger to his lips while closing the door. He steered the boy toward the television. "Let's unpack your meal, then find something for you to watch, okay?"

"Okay." Aaron knelt in front of the coffee table, waiting for him to place the chicken strips, French fries and carton of chocolate milk in front of him. The toy was a plastic lion, but Aaron pounced on it. "Mustafa!"

"Sure, kid." He had no clue who that was, but was grateful Aaron was happy. He found a children's channel on the television and gestured to the table. "Eat your food, okay?"

"Okay." Aaron chomped on a French fry.

Ryker sat on a chair near the door, instinctively taking the defensive position, and quickly ate his meal.

His phone vibrated, and he picked up Duncan's call. "Are you close?"

"Ten minutes. Do you need something to eat?"

"We're good. Just grabbed something from across the street. But pick up something for yourselves. Once you get here, we'll need to find a place to ditch the sedan. It's not safe to have it nearby."

"Okay, make that fifteen minutes, then, so we can swing by and get food."

"Not a problem." Ryker smiled as he disconnected from the call. It felt good to have backup so close.

"Ryker?" Olivia's sleepy voice came from the doorway. He swung around to face her, relieved that the color had returned to her cheeks. "I didn't hear you return."

"You needed the rest." He stood and gestured to a chair near Aaron. "Have a seat. I'll get your food."

"Thank you." She'd finished her meal by the time Duncan and Mike arrived.

"Thanks for coming, guys. Olivia, this is Duncan O'Hare and Mike Callahan." He gestured to the two men. "Duncan is a cop and former soldier who served with me in Afghanistan, but Mike is just a cop." He cocked a brow toward Mike, letting him know he was teasing.

"Just a cop." Mike let out a snort. "Gee, thanks. It's nice to meet you, Olivia."

"Yes, it is," Duncan chimed in. "Ryker, are you ready to roll out to ditch the car?"

"Sure." He gestured toward Mike. "Would you mind staying here with Olivia and Aaron?"

"Are you sure you trust me? After all, I'm just a private investigator turned cop."

"Yeah, I trust you." One of the things Ryker had missed after leaving the army was this brotherly ribbing. Having no siblings of his own, he'd enjoyed the camaraderie of the men who'd fought beside him. "We won't be long."

"I think I can handle it," Mike said dryly.

Ryker nodded at Olivia before leaving the motel. He drove the tan sedan to a strip mall he'd remembered seeing on the way in. Leaving the car behind gave him a measure of satisfaction.

One less way for the Blake-Moore Group to track them down.

Back at the motel, he drew the two men aside to fill them in on everything that had taken place in the past twenty-four hours.

"Blake-Moore strikes again." Mike scowled. "Hawk I could understand. After all, he'd witnessed a crime. But coming after a pregnant woman and her son? What kind of threat are they?"

"I don't know." Ryker glanced between the two men. "I'd like to move again tonight, but Olivia is exhausted. I'm afraid to push her too far. If she goes into premature labor…"

Duncan and Mike exchanged a glance. "I think we're safe here," Duncan said. "We're armed. We can take care of anything that comes up."

"Yeah. That's good." Ryker relaxed for what felt like the first time in hours. His head still throbbed, as did the wound on his thigh, but he didn't care. "I need to hit the shower and get a couple hours of sleep, but I can take the second watch."

"Go." Duncan waved a hand. "I've got first watch and Mike can take the second watch. You're no good to us if you're not one hundred percent."

Ryker nodded, knowing they were right.

A hot shower did wonders to ease his pain. The wound on his thigh didn't look too terrible. If it got worse, he'd pick up gauze and antibacterial ointment.

He fell into a deep sleep, secure in the knowledge that Mike and Duncan were watching over things.

But then a loud thudding noise brought him upright. He blinked, trying to get his bearings.

Another thud, then a muffled shout. He shot off the bed and grabbed his weapon.

Blake-Moore had found them!

SEVEN

A thud woke Olivia from a sound sleep. Had someone fallen? She pried open her eyes and peered at the cheap alarm clock on the night-stand.

Two in the morning. She glanced down at Aaron who was curled next to her. The noise hadn't woken him.

Another thud and a muffled shout sent fear spiking through her body. What in the world was going on?

She slid out of bed, steadying herself with a hand on the wall. Her bladder urged her toward the bathroom, but before she could take a step, she heard a sharp report.

A gunshot?

No! Please, Lord, help us! She bent over and scooped Aaron into her arms, although she wasn't sure where to go or what to do. Where was Ryker? Duncan? Mike?

She had no weapon of any sort. Not that she'd

know what to do with one anyway. There was a bathroom within the suite, so she went inside, locked the door and glanced around, her thoughts whirling.

The Blake-Moore Group must have found her. Again. She wanted to cry, to rant and scream in frustration, but forced herself to swallow the cries burning the back of her throat.

Think. *Think!* Her gaze landed on the toilet. The motel hadn't been updated in years, and the toilet tank was similar to the one she had at home, with a heavy ceramic cover on it.

"Mommy?" Aaron raised his head, rubbing at his eyes.

"Shh. We have to be quiet." Olivia set him down in the bathtub, the safest place she could think of. "Stay here, okay?"

"I don't wanna." His lower lip trembled and she was very much afraid that he'd begin wailing at any moment.

She lifted her heart in prayer. *God, please protect us!*

"Mommy?" Her son lifted his arms toward her, his gaze begging.

"Shh. Please, Aaron. I need you to be quiet. We don't want the bad guys to find us." She hated scaring him but was more worried about what would happen if he cried loud enough to draw attention. She quickly lifted the heavy porcelain cover off the tank and held it over her head, positioning herself behind the door.

If anyone came inside, she'd whack him over the head, hopefully with enough force to knock him unconscious.

Time passed in slow motion. The noises coming from the main suite area concerned her. What if something happened to Mike and Duncan?

To Ryker?

Her heart squeezed painfully in her chest and her arm muscles quivered beneath the weight of the toilet tank lid. She blinked back tears, trying to convince herself that Ryker would survive.

That they would *all* survive.

"Olivia? Are you in there?" Ryker's familiar voice made her knees go weak.

Thank You, God!

"Yes, we're in the bathroom." She lowered the lid of the toilet tank and moved out from behind the door. After setting the tank cover back in place, she opened the door, grateful beyond belief to see Ryker standing there. "What happened? Is everyone all right?"

"Yeah, but we need to hit the road." His face was drawn into tight lines, his gaze grim. "Now."

"They found us?" Silly question, since she knew they must have. "How?"

Ryker slowly shook his head. "They must have followed us. I didn't see them, but they must have had a line on our vehicle. Get your things together."

"Okay." She didn't need to be told twice. She quickly used the bathroom, then carried Aaron back into the bedroom. Her zebra bag was in the main living space, and she only had the one set of clothes, so there wasn't anything to grab other than Aaron's plastic lion and toy plane.

When she stepped into the suite, she stopped abruptly, her gaze landing on the two men dressed in black lying on the floor. One of them was bleeding badly; the other didn't show any signs of blood.

"Are they dead?" She couldn't help asking.

"Just one of them." Ryker's voice was low and harsh, as if it pained him to know that one of the men had died.

Mike and Duncan were tying the wrists of the guy who wasn't bleeding. The man let out a low moan and she knew then that he'd only been knocked out.

Not dead. Like the other.

Nausea swirled and she did her best to stave it off. Ryker had the zebra bag over his shoulder, watching as Mike and Duncan hauled the guy up and into a chair.

Ryker leaned close. "Who sent you?"

The man stirred, but didn't say a word. His eyes remained closed, and she couldn't tell if he was only pretending or if he was semiconscious.

Ryker gave him a hard shake. "Wake up! Who sent you?"

Still nothing. The man's eyes remained shut, his head lolling to the side. She felt sick, realizing he likely had a head injury of some sort.

Which wasn't good, but was better than being dead.

Mike and Duncan stood back, watching, their expressions grim. She shifted Aaron in her arms. "Come on, Ryker. Let's just go."

He ignored her. "What does Blake-Moore want with Olivia?" he asked the intruder.

"Nuther." The word was mumbled in a way that made it difficult for her to understand. The man's eyes were still closed, but he frowned as if confused about what was happening.

"Nothing? Don't tell me nothing. Why are you here?" Ryker shook him again. "What do you want with her?"

"Nub…ber…" His voice trailed off again, his jaw hanging slack.

If it was an act, it was a good one. Her stomach swirled again and she had to swallow hard to stop from throwing up.

"Ryker, we need to get out of here." Duncan stepped forward. "They could have called for additional support from the mercenary group. Or the noise may have drawn attention from the local police. We can't stick around."

"Fine." Ryker left the man on the chair and stood, raking a hand over his hair. "Let's go."

Liv headed toward the door, but Ryker stopped her with a hand on her arm. His voice was kind now. "Let me carry Aaron."

"All right." She handed her son over. By this time, Aaron was used to being in Ryker's arms and didn't protest.

Instead, her little boy snuggled against Ryker's chest, sucking on his thumb again, as if instinctively knowing he was safer there with Ryker than anywhere else.

Duncan led the way outside. Ryker remained behind Duncan, with Mike covering her back. She wasn't sure what she'd do if they came upon other men from the Blake-Moore Group. How much more could they take?

She straightened her spine and shook off the overwhelming sense of despair. They were alive, which was the most important thing right now.

She felt humbled to realize Ryker and his friends had risked their lives to keep her and Aaron safe.

Just as he'd promised they would.

"Get in." Ryker held the passenger door of

a black SUV open for her. She glanced in the back, relieved to see Aaron's car seat was already buckled in.

Moments later, Ryker slid behind the wheel. He gestured for Mike and Duncan to roll out first, in an identical SUV, then followed them.

"Are you sure you're okay?" She reached out and lightly rested her hand on his forearm. His skin was warm beneath her fingertips. "I heard a lot of noise."

"I'm fine." His words were clipped and she realized he was angry. "I should have moved from the motel as soon as we ditched the sedan."

"If they had followed us from the dealership, they likely would have followed again."

He let out a heavy sigh. "Thankfully, they must not have realized I had Duncan and Mike with me. I'm sure if they'd known, they would have come with more men."

More men. She shivered despite the warm June night air. It was horrifying to think that there would be more men coming after them.

Forever, or at least until they'd gotten what they'd wanted.

Whichever came first.

"Why had he said *nothing* in response to your question?" Olivia's voice interrupted his dark thoughts. "If he was only partially conscious, you'd think he'd spill the truth."

"Blake-Moore must have used some heavy-duty training to have them answer that way." He paused, then added, "Although, I thought he said numbers."

"Numbers?" She looked at him in horror. "You know I'm an accountant, right?"

No, he hadn't known that. He glanced at her. "Did you do accounting work for Blake-Moore?"

"No." She rubbed her hand over her belly and he knew she was troubled by what had gone down at the motel. Duncan had pulled the trigger, killing the first mercenary, but it may as well have been him. "I offered, but Tim refused my help. Said the bosses wanted a big-shot accounting firm to help manage their funds."

"Interesting." Ryker watched the taillights of the SUV in front of them. "So you wouldn't know of any numbers they might be looking for?"

"No idea. Hey, I thought we were heading toward Milwaukee?"

The Peoria sign had caught her attention. "We will, but I think it's better to stop for what's left of the night."

"It's because of me, isn't it?" Her voice was a bit shaky, and he again wished she hadn't had to witness so much violence. "I'll be fine if we need to drive longer."

He flashed a reassuring smile. "It's no problem. I need to discuss our strategy with Mike and Duncan anyway."

"If you're sure?"

"Positive." Ryker kept his eye on the taillights of Duncan's SUV. Olivia didn't say anything as they drove through the darkness. When he caught sight of a motel that offered suites, he flashed his lights.

Duncan tapped the breaks, signaling he understood, and slowed down so they could pull into the parking lot.

"Connecting suites?" Duncan asked from the driver's-side window.

"Yes." He stayed where he was, letting Duncan get the rooms this time. He thought about the dead man they'd left behind. Ryker figured the police would be on his tail thanks to the credit card information he'd had to provide in order to get the room. A wave of frustration washed over him. Having the police and the Blake-Moore Group after him would only complicate things. Good thing he had a couple of cops with him, to help corroborate his side of the story.

There was nothing he could do about it now. Olivia and Aaron needed to be safe. He could only hope that the guy Mike had knocked out would stay tied up and unconscious until the authorities arrived.

When Duncan emerged five minutes later, Ryker waited for his friends to open the rooms before sliding out from behind the wheel. He fetched the diaper bag and carefully lifted a sleeping Aaron from the car seat. Olivia went first, and he placed a hand on the lower part of her back, steering her toward the room on the left.

Inside, she turned the lamp on low.

"Where do you want him?" His voice was a low whisper.

"This way." She crossed over and pulled the covers down so that he could gently place Aaron on the bed. She stared at her son for a long moment and he wondered what was going through her mind.

Guilt stabbed him deep. Security was his specialty, he should have been more careful. He should have been able to figure out they were being followed.

He'd nearly gotten Olivia and Aaron killed.

Backing out of the bedroom, he returned to the living room of the suite. He double-checked the dead bolt on the door, then hooked the chain as an added measure. He dropped the diaper bag onto a chair. The connecting door between the suites was open, but he didn't hear Mike or Duncan.

"What kind of strategy?"

Olivia's soft voice had him spinning toward her. He'd assumed she would have crawled in beside Aaron, to get the sleep she badly needed.

He shrugged, striving for a casual tone. "Just a plan for where to go from here. Nothing to worry about." He hated knowing she was chin deep in this mess as it was. The last thing he wanted to do was cause additional stress.

She rubbed her hands on her arms as if she were chilled. "I keep thinking about the guy saying *numbers*."

He moved closer, fighting the urge to pull her into his arms. "You think you know what numbers he's talking about?"

She grimaced and shook her head. "I wish. If I had them, I'd gladly give them away."

No way was he going to allow her to do anything of the kind. If the Blake-Moore Group was willing to kill for the numbers, then Ryker knew they had to do with something illegal.

Money laundering? Or money socked away from their scheme of selling guns to the enemy?

"I'm scared." Olivia's soft admission was like a punch to his gut. "Oh!" She put a hand on her belly. "Sure, now the baby wakes up."

His fingers itched to feel the baby's movements, but he kept his hands at his sides. He wondered if his longing had shown on his face, because she unexpectedly grabbed his hand and put it on her belly.

"Can you feel it?"

"Yes." Feeling the baby move filled him with awe. The intimacy of the moment was humbling, and he was honored she'd shared this with him. "Amazing."

"It is, isn't it?" She smiled. "Thank you, Ryker. For everything you're doing for me. For us."

His throat swelled with emotion. Her gratitude was misplaced, but he also knew that if he hadn't tracked her down when he did, the outcome would have been much worse.

"You're welcome." He forced the words through his tight throat. "Get some sleep. I'm going to talk to Mike and Duncan to figure out how we can drop off the Blake-Moore Group's radar."

She nodded, but didn't move away. She continued covering his hand on her belly with hers, as if she didn't want to let go.

Unable to help himself, he reached up and tucked a strand of dark hair behind her ear with his other hand. "I'm going to do everything possible to keep you and Aaron safe." The baby kicked again, making him smile. "Him, too."

"Her." Olivia's lips curved in a smile. "This pregnancy is very different, so I'm thinking the baby is a girl."

Since he knew nothing about it, he didn't argue. "Her, then. I'm going to keep all three of you safe."

"I know you will." Her trust leveled him. "I know God sent you to help us, Ryker, guiding us on His chosen path."

He stilled, her simple faith washing over him. Was she right about God? Was He really watching over them, guiding them to safety? The Callahans believed that, as did Hawk.

Were they right?

"Ryker." She let go of his hand, shifting closer. He told himself to back off, to give her room, but his boots didn't move. She leaned forward, resting her head in the crook of his shoulder. "I'm blessed to have you here with us."

Blessed? If either one of them was blessed, it was him. He couldn't think of a response, so he simply lowered his head and pressed a chaste kiss on her temple.

She lifted her head to gaze up at him. He wished he could see her eyes more clearly, but the lack of light made it difficult to observe beyond the shadows.

"Is something wrong?" He didn't know what

she was thinking, or why she continued looking up at him.

"Nothing." A smile curved her lips and she surprised him by reaching up to wrap her hand around his neck. Then she gently pulled him down as she went up on her tiptoes.

It never occurred to him to resist. She kissed him. Sweetly at first, but then with a longing that he couldn't ignore or deny.

He wrapped his arms around her, pulling her close and deepening the kiss, the way he'd wanted to since they'd first met. She tasted like sunshine and wildflowers after the rain. He wanted nothing more than to keep holding her, but the baby kicked between them, and he couldn't help but laugh.

"Well, I'm not sure my kiss has ever spurred that reaction," she said with a wry smile.

"It's beautiful and so are you." He was about to kiss her again when he heard a small voice call out, "Mommy?"

Aaron's plaintive cry made Olivia sigh. "I'm sorry but I need to go to him."

"I know." He reluctantly loosened his grip. "Get some sleep. We'll talk in the morning."

She nodded, turned and rushed to Aaron's bedside. He listened as she reassured the little boy. Peering through the open doorway, he saw her cuddling the child close. His chest ached as he watched them.

It was a full minute before he could make himself move away from the doorway, her taste lingering on his lips.

She'd kissed him, but now that the cloud of attraction had faded, he knew he shouldn't read too much into their embrace. She'd been scared, had hidden in the bathroom with a toilet tank cover as a weapon. The stress of being on the run for her life, was probably getting to her. Coming to him for comfort didn't mean anything.

He couldn't let it mean anything.

Getting emotionally involved wasn't smart. He needed his wits about him to figure out how to stop the Blake-Moore Group, while keeping her and Aaron safe.

Another lapse in judgment on his part could prove deadly.

EIGHT

Had she lost her mind? Why on earth had she kissed Ryker? He'd been trying to comfort her, the way any friend might after running from bad guys with guns, but she'd turned a sweet embrace into something romantic.

Long after Aaron had fallen asleep, she'd replayed those moments over and over in her mind.

It's beautiful and so are you.

Just remembering the words made her shiver with awareness. An attraction she hadn't felt in a very long time.

It was impossible not to compare Ryker and Tim. Her husband had lost interest in her while she'd been pregnant with Aaron. At the time, she'd blamed his new job with Blake-Moore for the long hours Tim had spent away from home. Blamed it for his short temper and the subtle changes she'd noticed in his demeanor.

But deep down, she'd feared her husband was

becoming a stranger. No matter how much she tried to find the man she'd married, he'd remained elusive. She'd attempted to rejuvenate their relationship, hoping that reconnecting with him on an intimate level would bring life back to his eyes, but it hadn't worked. She believed Blake-Moore was to blame.

Those instincts had proven correct, based on the way the Blake-Moore Group had sent armed men after her.

Only after Tim's death had she really understood that her marriage would not have survived a second pregnancy. That their relationship was damaged beyond repair.

She hadn't even had the chance to tell Tim about the baby. Frankly, she'd been afraid of his reaction. Then it had been too late.

Not that it mattered now. The relief of knowing she wouldn't have to deal with Tim made her feel guilty. He'd been her husband, a man she'd once loved. But he'd eventually turned into someone else.

A man she didn't recognize.

Which brought her back to Ryker. Sweet, caring, strong, compassionate Ryker.

It was crazy. She was getting in way over her head. Telling herself this was nothing more than some strange hero worship didn't help.

As much as she appreciated Duncan's and

Mike's help, her senses were only tuned in to Ryker. A man she had no business kissing. Or wanting.

The minute she and Aaron were out of danger, Ryker would move on to his next project. Whatever that might be.

She didn't know much of anything about his personal life, other than he worked as a security specialist. But what about the women in his life? Or his family? She had no idea.

Exhaustion finally shut down her brain long enough to sleep.

The following morning, she woke up feeling well rested. But the serene feeling of hope quickly evaporated when she realized Aaron wasn't beside her.

"Aaron?" She rolled off the bed, her heart hammering in her chest. She yanked the bedroom door open and saw Ryker had Aaron on his lap, feeding him something they must have gotten from a nearby restaurant.

"He's fine. We tried not to wake you, right, champ?" Ryker grinned down at the boy.

"Right." The words were muffled by the food in her son's mouth.

"Thank you." Her panic faded and she drew a hand through her tousled hair, suddenly feeling self-conscious about her appearance. She'd been wearing the same maternity clothes for the past two days. Ugh.

The kiss they'd shared hovered in the air between them.

"We have something for you, too," Ryker added, avoiding her direct gaze. "When you're ready, let us know."

"Okay." She desperately needed the bathroom and a shower, in that order. Ducking back into the bedroom, she closed the door and made use of the facilities. It was nice to have a few minutes to herself. Normally Aaron talked to her through the shower curtain as she showered.

Another reason to like Ryker.

Enough. This idiotic preoccupation with the man had to stop. She'd obviously made him uncomfortable with her kiss. Not that she could blame him. Her hormones were raging out of control—it was the only explanation for why she was acting so strangely.

Wrinkling her nose, she dressed in the same clothes she'd been wearing the night Ryker had rescued her from the man on the street. Maybe once they were safe, she'd be able to stop and pick up a few things.

She returned to the living room of the suite. The scent of bacon and eggs made her stomach rumble. Aaron had finished eating, and was sitting in front of the television.

"Aaron, do you need to go to the bathroom?" She approached, sniffing the air around him to see if he had soiled his pants. He normally wore Pull-Ups at night, but was potty trained during the day.

Although after everything that had happened, she wouldn't be surprised if he regressed.

"No. Mr. Ryker already helped me." Aaron didn't look away from the cartoon.

She lifted a brow and turned toward Ryker who shrugged. "Wasn't hard to find what I needed in your bag."

He'd changed Aaron? Wow. "Thank you." She crossed over and took a seat beside him. Opening the to-go container, she found scrambled eggs, bacon and hash browns. She was thankful for the food. "Looks great."

"Dig in." A smile tugged at the corner of Ryker's mouth.

She took several bites of her meal before realizing Mike and Duncan weren't around, although the connecting door between the rooms hung ajar. "Where are the guys?"

"They'll be here soon." Ryker's smile faded. "We're trying to drum up additional reinforcements, but so far there's no one else to spare."

Additional reinforcements? Another wave of guilt washed over her.

She'd just finished her breakfast when Mike

walked in. "Sorry, no go. Noah is busy with Maddy and their new son. Matt doesn't want to leave Lacy as she's due any day now. Marc is out of town until tomorrow, and Miles is knee-deep in a murder case."

The names were a blur, and Ryker must have noticed her confusion.

"Mike has five siblings," he explained. "And they're all involved in some sort of law enforcement. Marc is with the FBI, Miles is a homicide detective, Matt is a K-9 cop, Noah is a cop and married to their sister, Maddy, who is an ADA." Ryker frowned. "What about Mitch?"

Mike shrugged. "He's an arson investigator, but he and Dana are vacationing in Door County. It's possible Mitch may be able to help when they return."

"Wow, six Callahans." She glanced at Duncan who'd come in behind Mike. "And you're Mike's brother-in-law."

"Yep. Mike married my sister Shayla." He clapped Mike on the shoulder. "And from what I hear, they're about to make me an uncle again."

The tips of Mike's ears turned red, but he nodded and smiled broadly, clearly happy with the news. "Not until November, though."

"Congrats." Ryker gave Mike a nod. "I'm happy for you."

"Thanks."

It was oddly reassuring to Olivia to have so many family men helping them. They no doubt understood what it was like to travel with a pregnant woman and a small child.

Mike's expression turned serious. "Actually, I think we should all hit the road as soon as we can. Shayla told me Brodie has been throwing up nonstop all night. She hasn't been feeling very good herself, either."

"Poor kid." Duncan frowned. "Fine with me if we leave, the sooner we get back in Wisconsin the better. We have a good two and a half hours of driving before we reach the Wisconsin border, and another seventy minutes to get to Madison."

"I plan to detour to Milwaukee rather than going all the way to Madison." Mike sent Ryker an apologetic look. "I'll ask Miles to pick me up in Beloit, so I won't take you out of your way. But I really need to check on Shayla and Brodie, to make sure they're okay."

"Understood." If Ryker was upset about losing Mike and having only Duncan as backup, he didn't show it.

"I can be ready in five minutes." She stood and quickly cleaned up the mess from their breakfast. "Just let me stop in the bathroom one last time."

When she returned a few minutes later, she found Ryker and Duncan deep in conversation.

"We need to confront the cousin." Ryker's voice held a note of urgency. "He lives outside Madison, so it's on the way."

"Yeah, maybe. Although I still think we should check out the Habush house first. Could be that the numbers they're looking for may be hidden in there."

"Doubtful. They would have searched the place already," Ryker argued.

Duncan caught sight of her and stood. "Hey, Olivia. Ready?"

"Yes." She glanced at Ryker who looked sheepish at being overheard. "Are you really going to talk to Tim's cousin Seth Willis?"

Ryker exchanged a wary look with Duncan before nodding. "Yeah, that's the plan. But we have several hours of driving to do before we're even close, so let's not worry about that now."

She frowned, not liking the way he was keeping her out of the loop. "What else do you have planned?"

Ryker sighed. "Nothing. Seth is the only lead we have, other than the word *number*—if that's even what the mercenary mumbled while he was out of it." She saw the hint of frustration in his gaze. "If you're ready, let's go."

She packed Aaron's few things in the diaper

bag. Ryker took the bag from her and slung it over his shoulder, then held out his hands for Aaron.

Her son went to him easily, and she was struck again by how much Ryker had become an important part of their world in such a short amount of time.

Her heart squeezed as she silently admitted how much she'd miss him once this was over.

Ryker kept his gaze on the road, his thoughts whirling. He didn't like knowing he'd only have Duncan's help for the next leg of their journey. Still, he didn't begrudge the Callahans the need to support their spouses and children. He would do exactly the same thing if the situation was reversed.

But he'd hoped to surround Olivia and Aaron with armed men who could look after her while he worked the case.

"You really think he said the word *number*?"

Olivia's voice pulled him from his thoughts.

"Yeah, I do. Mike and Duncan agreed, especially once they learned you were an accountant."

"But I didn't do any accounting work for Blake-Moore."

"I know." It would have made things easier for them if she had. The way things stood now she didn't have access or any reason to be connected to Blake-Moore's accounts.

Except through her dead husband and brother.

And what about the numbers, anyway? Why had numbers sent men searching for Olivia? Was it possible she had information she wasn't aware of? He glanced at her. "You don't happen to have a key to a safe-deposit box or anything in that diaper bag of yours, do you?"

She frowned. "No, of course not."

He'd been in the bag several times and hadn't seen anything out of the ordinary. Yet he hadn't done a full inventory of the contents, either. Something to consider once they reached their next destination.

His gaze flicked to the rearview mirror. This time, he was in the lead with Mike and Duncan covering his six. He was grateful to have them behind him, and knew they'd keep an eye out for anyone following them. He kept his speed about five miles per hour over the speed limit, keeping up with the rest of the traffic heading north.

This way he could set the pace, or rather, Olivia could, as she was the one who needed frequent rest stops.

As they rolled into Rockford, she gestured toward a gas station. "Would you mind pulling in?"

"No problem." He tapped the brake, letting

Mike and Duncan know that they were stopping. The SUV behind them slowed, then followed them into the gas station.

Mike pulled up to a gas pump and jumped out of the car. "May as well fill up."

"Okay." He pulled in behind him, then slid out from behind the wheel. "I'll go inside with Olivia and Aaron first."

"I'll fill it up for you." Duncan waved him off.

"Thanks." He lifted Aaron out of his car seat, then followed Olivia inside. She had the diaper bag, and he wondered if he should look through it now or wait until later.

Olivia took Aaron's hand and led him into the restroom.

Okay, later then. He stayed near the door, but positioned himself so that he could also keep an eye on the gas pumps through the window. Duncan and Mike didn't speak, their gazes alert on the cars coming and going around them.

They were good friends and he was fortunate they'd dropped everything to come help.

"We're much better now. Thanks."

Olivia's voice had him turning toward her. He'd been so preoccupied he hadn't heard her and Aaron come out. "All set?"

"I wanna toy!" Aaron hopped from one foot to the next. "Please, Mommy?"

She sighed. "No, Aaron. You can't get a toy every time we stop to use the restroom."

"I don't mind—" Ryker stopped when she narrowed her gaze at him.

"No. Not now. Maybe later," she told her son. She took Aaron's hand in hers, but he pulled away.

"I wanna toy!" By the looks of it, the kid was gearing up for a full-blown temper tantrum.

"No." Olivia looked tired and stressed, not that Ryker blamed her. But she ignored Aaron's cries, took him by the hand and dragged him toward the door.

Feeling helpless, he trailed behind them. Aaron dug in his heels yanking Olivia off-balance. He swooped the boy into his arms and strode outside.

"Enough." His stern tone surprised Aaron, and he stopped crying.

He gently set the boy in the car seat and buckled him in. The kid was still crying, but not nearly as out of control as he had been. When he glanced over at Olivia, she offered a weary smile. "Thanks."

"You're welcome." He hated the idea of her dealing with Aaron on her own, especially in her condition.

Sweeping his gaze over the gas station, he looked for anything out of place.

Nothing. Aaron's crying hadn't drawn much attention, either. Guess that wasn't unusual when it came to kids.

Yet, he felt unsettled, the back of his neck tingling with warning. It wasn't over yet. He slid behind the wheel, eager to get back on the road. Mike and Duncan let him pull out first, then followed.

"We'll be at the Wisconsin border soon." He could tell by the toll station looming up ahead. "Beloit is only thirty miles from here."

"Good, I guess." She looked hesitant about returning to Madison as she rested her hands on her abdomen. "I'll be sorry to see Mike go."

"We'll be okay." He infused confidence in his tone. He slowed to get through the toll, then increased his speed. The roads were wide open now, without much traffic. There weren't a lot of homes or businesses along this stretch of the highway and the prickly feeling wouldn't leave him alone.

He plucked his phone from the console between them and called Mike.

"What's up?" Mike's tone was on alert.

"Let's change the meeting spot to Delavan."

There was a pause. "Okay, any particular reason why?"

"It's smaller, easier to pick up a tail." Beloit

was a larger city, and he felt better about going to a smaller, contained area.

"Okay, I'll let Miles know." Mike hung up.

Olivia's gaze showed her concern. "You think they're still following us?"

"I don't know." And he didn't like the feeling of being in a fishbowl, where their two SUVs could be seen for miles. "Probably not."

She didn't relax, but grasped the hand rest on her door like a lifeline.

Several miles had passed by, when his phone rang. Olivia picked it up and put it on speaker. "What's wrong?"

"We've got company." Duncan's terse tone filled him with dread.

"How many?"

"Just one SUV that I can see. But we have to assume they have reinforcements nearby."

Farm fields stretched on either side of them, and Ryker second-guessed his decision to bypass Beloit for Delavan. But it was too late to change direction now. He pressed on the gas, increasing their speed. "Where's Miles? Can he meet us?"

"Yes, he's on his way. We'll take care of the tail. You get Olivia and Aaron to safety."

"Got it." He tightened his grip on the wheel. When he saw an abandoned field without crops, he knew it was the best option. "Hang on, we're going off-road."

"Off-road?" Her appalled echo was cut off as they bounced off the highway and headed straight through the empty field.

"Hang on." The vehicle bucked and rolled over rocks and chunks of earth. The four-wheel drive helped keep them steady, and he took the shortest route directly toward another road he could just barely see off in the distance.

He darted a quick glance at the rearview mirror. Mike and Duncan were farther back now, and he knew they would do whatever was necessary to keep the guys from Blake-Moore from coming after them.

The sound of gunfire had him clenching his teeth. He didn't normally pray, but it may be that the Callahans' and Hawk's faith was rubbing off on him, because he found himself asking for help and guidance now.

Lord, if You can hear me, please give me the strength I need to get Olivia and Aaron away from the Blake-Moore Group. Help me keep them safe!

NINE

Liv clutched the door handle in a tight grip, trying not to cry out at the way the SUV jolted and rolled over the dirt and rocks of the field. With the other hand, she held her stomach, as if willing the baby to stay put.

No premature labor. Please.

"Mommy!" Aaron's fearful cry stabbed her heart.

"Isn't this fun?" She glanced over her shoulder at her son and forced a reassuring smile. "Mr. Ryker is taking us four-wheeling."

"No! Don't wanna go four whee-ing." Aaron's lower lip trembled and he tucked his thumb into his mouth, a sure sign he was upset. "I'm scared."

"It's okay. There's no reason to be scared. Mr. Ryker is getting us to safety." A quick glance at Ryker's grim expression was not reassuring. "How about we sing nursery rhymes?"

Aaron seemed to consider her idea then

plucked his thumb from his mouth. "Humpty-dumpty sat on a wall," he sang.

"Humpty-dumpty had a great fall," she chimed in.

Ryker raised a brow, but didn't interrupt their singing as they finished the nursery rhyme. She was glad to see the highway was getting closer now, and thought it was possible that he'd make it to safety.

Pop! Pop!

Liv sucked in a harsh breath and turned to look through the back window. The men from Blake-Moore were shooting at them? An SUV that looked much like the one they were using had followed them onto the field.

Why wouldn't they just leave her alone?

Because of the numbers? Numbers she didn't know anything about. She didn't understand. It didn't make any sense.

Ryker's jaw was tight as he pressed harder on the gas, the SUV swaying even more as he obviously tried to shake off whoever was following them.

And what about Duncan and Mike? Were they okay? Or had the Blake-Moore Group gotten to them? She closed her eyes and prayed for all of them.

Dear Lord, help us! Protect us! Show us the way out!

Time seemed to move in slow motion. Each jerky, rocky movement of the SUV made her feel sick to her stomach. She prayed she wouldn't throw up her breakfast.

Then abruptly, Ryker reached the end of the field, going up and over the ditch to the highway. The moment the SUV was on level ground, he hit the gas hard, going from fifteen miles per hour to fifty, then more.

"Mommy, let's sing another one."

Her son's request helped keep her from screaming in frustration. She darted a glance behind them, realizing the pursuing SUV was far back, still in the field.

"Hey, how about 'Three Blind Mice'?" Ryker's suggestion had her gaping at him in surprise.

"Three blind mice, three blind mice," Aaron sang. "See how they run. See how they run."

When Ryker joined in, tears pricked at her eyes. He was so understanding, so sweet. So kind and gentle toward her and Aaron.

She didn't know what she'd do without him.

Ryker didn't let up on the gas for several miles. When Aaron grew tired of the nursery rhymes, Ryker handed her his phone.

"See if you can reach Duncan."

Her fingers were slick from sweat, but she managed to call Duncan, placing the phone on speaker. Her throat grew tight as the phone rang several times without an answer.

Finally, she heard Duncan's voice asking, "Are you safe?"

"Yeah, for now." Ryker glanced again at the rearview mirror. "But I think both of our vehicles have been compromised."

"Ya think?" Duncan's droll tone almost made her smile. "We'll stick with the plan to meet in Delavan for now. We'll find a way to get new wheels once we get there."

There was a moment of hesitation before Ryker agreed. "Yeah, sounds good. You and Mike are okay, too?"

"Yep. We took out their tires. Should slow them down."

"Thanks. We'll be in touch." Ryker turned his attention back to the highway.

She blinked. "You mean, that was Duncan and Mike shooting? Not the Blake-Moore Group?"

He met her gaze for a brief moment. "I was hoping so."

She slumped in her seat as relief washed over her. "I thought—" She abruptly stopped, glancing back at Aaron.

"I know. I'm sorry." Ryker reached over to take her hand in his. "The good news is that we managed to get away unscathed."

"Yes." She had to force the word past her constricted throat. He was right, and she knew God was continuing to watch over them.

But those moments when she feared a bullet would find its way into the car, hitting Aaron or Ryker, had been awful.

Her stomach cramped and she gasped and held her breath, rubbing her fingertips over her belly in a soothing manner. Stress was bad for the baby.

They'd been under stress pretty much nonstop over the past three days. And she had a horrible feeling the ongoing stress wasn't about to end anytime soon.

"Olivia?" A hint of fear threaded Ryker's tone. "What's wrong?"

"Nothing. We're fine." She did her best to sound confident, even though she was anything but. "Everything is fine."

Ryker's gaze was skeptical and she knew he didn't believe her. But she refused to consider the prospect of being in premature labor.

No way. Uh-uh. Not happening.

Ryker fell silent, although ripples of concern emanated off him like heat waves. Ignoring his negative energy, she continued to concentrate on breathing deeply, in and out, while smoothing her hands over her belly. The odd cramping sensation faded away. After a full ten minutes, she decided there was nothing to worry about.

She and the baby were fine.

The sign for Delavan indicated they were only ten minutes away. For once, she didn't need to use the restroom and hoped they could switch vehicles quickly and get out of town, before anyone from the Blake-Moore Group caught up to them.

She longed to feel safe. To not constantly glance over her shoulder to see if anyone was behind them.

Was it too much to ask to bring her baby into a secure world where danger didn't lurk behind every corner?

The depths of despair pulled at her, and she did her best to shove it aside.

Willa had told her several times that God helps those who help themselves. Now that they'd been found for the fourth time in less than three days, she needed desperately to keep believing that God was watching over them.

She couldn't give up. Not now, and maybe not ever. If she needed to change her identity and disappear for good, then fine.

That's exactly what she'd do.

It would be worth starting over under a new identity in order to have the safety and security she needed to raise her family.

* * *

Ryker was thankful that Mike and Duncan had bought him time to escape the mercenaries. Yet the fact that they kept coming was gravely concerning.

Whatever they wanted from Olivia was big. Big enough to risk losing several good—if misguided—men in order to get it back.

As they came into the town of Delavan, he slowed his speed, unwilling to draw undue attention from the locals. His goal was for the three of them to look like a happy little family.

And if his chest tightened at the thought of having a family of his own, he ignored it.

Glancing around the quaint town, he tried to think of a way to ditch their current SUVs for something untraceable. As much as they'd managed to stay one step ahead of the Blake-Moore Group, if by the skin of their teeth, he didn't like the way they kept showing up.

Especially knowing they wouldn't stop until they had what they wanted. Which meant he needed to find it first. Whatever it was.

His phone rang, and he handed it to Olivia, who put the call on speaker. "Yeah?"

"We're about ten minutes out of Delavan. Miles is bringing an unmarked SUV to a small restaurant called the Early Bird Café." Duncan's voice was calm and steady. Ryker was relieved to have a fellow soldier with him. "We'll meet there, but you'll want to park the SUV a good distance from the restaurant."

"What's the ETA for Miles?" He glanced around as he headed into the downtown area, searching for the café. It was located on the corner of Main and Birch streets.

"Hopefully ten to fifteen minutes."

"I see the café." He drove past it, looking for a good spot to leave the SUV. "We'll see you there."

"Will do." Duncan disconnected from the call.

"Where are you planning to leave the car?" Olivia's voice held a note of uncertainty.

"Not sure." He turned right on the opposite side of Main Street. When he saw a small police station, he grinned and gestured toward it. "There."

"Won't the police be all over an abandoned SUV?" Olivia looked apprehensive.

"Under normal circumstances, yes, but with Duncan's and Mike's connections to the Milwaukee Police Department and Sheriff's Department we can get the locals to let the SUV sit for a while."

She didn't look convinced. He pulled into the parking lot, then slid out from behind the wheel. After looping the zebra-striped bag over his shoulder, he unbuckled Aaron and lifted the boy into his arms.

"I wanna walk." The kid squirmed in his arms, and he glanced at Olivia. She wearily nodded.

It went against the grain, but he bent over to set the child on his feet. Then he reached into the back and quickly unlatched the car seat. He knew Miles had a daughter and a son of his own, but wasn't sure he'd thought ahead to bring a car seat for Aaron.

He took one of Aaron's hands in his, Olivia took the other, and the three of them walked toward Main Street.

Like your average, everyday family.

He hoped.

The walk to the café seemed to take forever. He breathed a tiny sigh of relief when they entered the restaurant. After choosing a table toward the back, sitting so that he could face the doorway, they settled in to wait.

Duncan and Mike arrived first, dropping into chairs on either side of him.

"Thanks again," he said. "I appreciate you watching my back."

Duncan waved him off. "You'd do the same for us. Coffee, please," he added as the server approached.

Breakfast was only a couple of hours ago,

but he thought it might be good for Olivia and Aaron to eat something. "Lunch menus, please."

"Not for me. I'm fine," Olivia protested.

"I want chocolate milk." Aaron shot a glance at his mother, who nodded.

When they all had something to drink, Duncan leaned forward. "Okay, so Miles is bringing a clean SUV, but I'm feeling like we need two sets of wheels. It worked pretty well to have us hanging behind to cover your back."

Ryker nodded. There was no denying the strategy had worked. "Maybe we can pick up something else later tonight."

"I can meet up with you later, after I check on Shayla and Brodie," Mike offered.

Ryker was touched, but knew that Mike belonged with his wife and son. "Focus on taking care of your family. We'll think of something."

The door opened and Miles Callahan walked in. Without hesitation, he made his way toward them. "What's going on? Mike wouldn't say much when he called."

Ryker quickly filled him in on the Blake-Moore Group and the way the mercenaries continued to come after them.

Miles let out a low whistle between his teeth. "You're deep in a hot mess."

"Exactly. I have to believe they've been tracking the vehicles we're using. Maybe they have connections who can get registration information through the DMV, since we've only used disposable cell phones for the past twenty-four hours. With a clean SUV, we should be able to shake the tail."

"I took the SUV from the Milwaukee PD undercover lot." Miles grinned. "It's untraceable to you, or to the police, as I changed the vehicle's status to damaged in the computer system. Should be safe enough."

"Good." For the first time in what seemed like forever, Ryker felt a sense of relief. "If you don't mind, I'd like to get going."

"Not a problem." Miles set the keys on the table. "It's parked around the corner across from the police station."

"That's where I left our car." Ryker picked up the keys. "Maybe you could put in a good word with the locals to leave it there for a while. Or have it towed somewhere out of sight."

"Will do." Miles glanced at his brother. "Guess we're taking the hot SUV back to Milwaukee, huh?"

"Hey, it may help be a diversion for Ryker and Duncan." Mike didn't seem concerned about the potential danger.

"Thanks again, Miles." Ryker rose to his feet. He helped Olivia stand, then tossed the zebra bag over his shoulder. "I owe you one."

"Nah." Miles waved him off. "You came to bail us out last year. It's only fair we return the favor."

Duncan picked up the car seat. Olivia took Aaron's hand and made a quick trip to the restroom before they headed outside. Ryker led the way, with Duncan covering their backs.

At the car there was no sign of anyone lurking around. Olivia volunteered to sit in the back near Aaron, which irked Ryker for some reason. Duncan rode shotgun, as Ryker slid behind the wheel. He kept a keen eye on the rearview mirror, but didn't relax until they were out of town and back on the highway. Avoiding the interstate, he took the less traveled highway toward Whitewater, which would eventually get them to Madison.

"Where do you want to stay for the night?" Duncan asked.

"Somewhere remote and outside the Madison area, while being close enough to drive there as needed."

"Cambridge? We passed a sign. It's a few miles ahead and they have a motel."

"Just one motel?" He glanced at Duncan, who nodded. Great, just great. Although one motel was probably okay for now. He was hopeful that the mercenaries would assume they'd head to the Milwaukee area, rather than Madison.

Unless they already knew that Seth Willis was the lead they were following up on. He swallowed hard.

"Cambridge has beautiful hiking trails," Olivia said. "I've been there before."

"Okay, sounds like Cambridge is our next destination. Once we're settled in the motel, I need to drive out to do some recon on Tim's cousin." He glanced at Duncan. "I'd like you to stay back to watch over Olivia and Aaron."

"Wait, what? You're leaving?" Olivia's tone was sharp. "I'd rather come with you when you talk to Seth."

"No." His blunt, flat tone came out harsher than he intended, but he was tired, his head ached, the wound on his thigh burned and he was running out of patience. "I just managed to get you out of danger, Olivia. I'm not letting you step back into the middle of it."

"You don't understand, Ryker. Seth knows me. I think he'll talk more if I'm there to smooth things over." The stubborn streak he'd once found attractive was wearing thin.

He could feel Duncan's gaze on him, but thankfully his former army buddy didn't say anything. If he was honest, he'd admit leaving Olivia and Aaron with Duncan didn't sit well. It wasn't that he didn't trust Duncan, but every cell in his body shunned the idea of having Olivia out of his line of sight. Out of arm's reach.

He felt attached to her in a way that wasn't healthy. He wanted her to stay glued to his side, which was ridiculous. Wouldn't it be better to know she was safe with Duncan while he grilled Seth for inside information about the Blake-Moore Group?

Yes, it would. But he still didn't like it.

"Ryker? Did you hear me? Seth is more likely to cooperate if I'm there with you."

Duncan coughed and he speared him with a narrow look. "Olivia, please. I appreciate you want to help, but I don't think involving you and Aaron is smart. These men are playing a deadly game. And you're thirty-four weeks pregnant on top of that. I'm sorry, but you'll be better off staying at the motel with Duncan."

There was a long silence and he knew Olivia was trying to find a way to change his mind.

"I can always question Seth for you," Duncan offered.

It was tempting, very tempting to let Duncan take on the interrogation. But this was his problem, not Duncan's.

Actually, it was Olivia's problem, but that made it his problem. One he refused to let go. "No, I'd rather be the one to confront him. I'll feel much better knowing you're watching over Olivia and Aaron."

"Your call." Duncan was easygoing that way.

"Does it matter what I want?" Olivia's tone held an underlying note of panic. "Can't we just skip talking to Seth? I doubt he knows anything."

He caught her gaze in the rearview mirror. "Olivia, I need you to please trust me on this."

Her gaze pleaded with him to reconsider, and it was the hardest thing in the world to ignore it.

The kiss they'd shared still haunted him. He longed to kiss her again, and again.

Yep, he was in way over his head.

And the way things were going, he didn't think a life preserver would be tossed his way anytime soon.

TEN

Swallowing her frustration wasn't easy. Liv didn't want Ryker to leave her and Aaron with Duncan, so that he could confront Seth on his own. And for what? The slim chance of getting information?

It wasn't that she didn't trust Duncan's abilities to keep them safe. Without him and Mike covering for them in the field, they wouldn't have been able to escape. She owed both men a deep debt of gratitude.

Yet what she felt toward Ryker was different. She was in tune to him in a way that she didn't feel toward Duncan and Mike. She cared about him on a personal level. The very idea of him being harmed by Seth made her sick to her stomach.

The motel in Cambridge that Ryker identified for their next stop was in rough shape, a stark contrast to the pretty scenery. The neon vacancy sign had more letters burned out than lit. The paint on the building was faded and peeling, the shingles on the roof curling beneath the heat. She frowned, hoping the ceiling of their room didn't leak.

Duncan slid out of the passenger seat, then closed the door behind him with a solid thunk.

"Are we home?" Aaron asked.

Home. Her heart squeezed in her chest. It was a sad testament that she had no place to call home. "No, sweetie, we're staying in a motel. Won't that be fun?"

Her son wasn't buying her fake enthusiasm. "I don't wanna go to a motel. I wanna go home!"

"Aaron." Ryker's firm yet gentle tone caught her son's attention. Ryker turned in his seat so he could see the boy. "We can't go home until we're safe. No more complaining, okay? I'm sure there's a TV for you to watch, if your mom says it's okay."

Aaron eyed Ryker with a hint of confusion, as if he vaguely remembered what it was like to have a father, then surprised her by giving in. "Can I take my toys with me?"

"Of course." She sent Ryker a grateful smile. "And we'll find a movie for you to watch, too."

"With cars?" Her son's fascination with cars had made him badger her incessantly to play certain movies at home. She'd enjoyed watching it with him, although that seemed like a time in their lives that was far removed from where they were now.

"We'll see." She had no idea what sorts of movies were available and didn't want to make a promise she couldn't keep.

Duncan returned, getting back in the passenger seat. "We're all set. I have two connecting rooms at the end of the row. No suites here, I'm afraid."

"Thanks." Ryker put the car in gear and swung around toward the designated rooms. He pulled in and parked. "I don't like leaving the SUV out in the open like this. I'm going to park it behind the building."

"Good idea," Duncan agreed. He jumped out of the vehicle and quickly used the key to unlock the motel-room door.

Liv gathered Aaron's things from the SUV, tucking them in her diaper bag before she slid out. Ryker was already on the other side, extracting Aaron from his car seat.

The way he took on the fatherly tasks of caring for Aaron caused a lump to lodge in the back of her throat. It wasn't just that he didn't seem to mind, but more so that he took control of what needed to be done without being asked.

Almost as if he knew what it was like to have a child of his own.

She followed Ryker and Aaron into the motel

room, wrinkling her nose at the musty smell. She didn't say anything, but Ryker flipped a switch on the air-conditioning unit as if reading her mind.

"It will air out soon." He set Aaron on the floor.

"It's fine." In those first few nights she'd been on the run she'd stayed in worse places. No use complaining.

Being safe was all that mattered.

"Excuse me." She ducked into the bathroom for what seemed like the fiftieth time. The muted sounds of the television reached her ears, and she knew Ryker was getting Aaron settled. When she emerged a few minutes later, Aaron was watching *Cars* and Ryker was hovering near the connecting door between the rooms. She noticed his laptop was open and a picture of Seth Willis was up on the screen.

"I'll be back as soon as possible." Ryker met her gaze straight on. "If anything happens, Duncan will get you safely to the authorities."

"Please don't go." She wasn't proud of how pathetically desperate she sounded. "Duncan can question Seth just as easily as you can."

"No, Olivia. I'm the one responsible for getting to the bottom of this. Duncan has done more than enough for me."

By the stubborn glint in his eye she knew Ryker wasn't budging. She bit her lip. "Okay, but please be careful. Worrying about you will only add to my stress level."

Ryker's gaze dropped to her belly, then shifted away. She felt a pang of guilt at using her pregnancy as a way to convince him not to go. "This won't take long."

Ryker turned to leave. She rushed over and grasped his arm. "I'll pray for you."

He paused, then surprised her by nodding. "Thanks. At this point, I'll take all the prayers I can get."

He would? Surprised, she dropped her hand, and he swiftly moved through the connecting door and out to the SUV. Pushing away the edge of the curtain, she watched as he slid behind the wheel and drove away.

The SUV was nothing but a black speck on the horizon when she finally let the curtain drop. A peculiar warmth spread through her at the way Ryker had agreed to accept her prayers.

She hadn't found God and faith until she'd met Willa. And the idea of sharing her faith with a man was even more foreign. Her life before, with Tim, hadn't revolved around God.

But the knowledge that Ryker actually believed in the power of prayer reassured her in a way nothing else did.

God must have a plan for him. For *them*.

She just needed to be patient until she understood what that plan entailed.

Ryker hated leaving Olivia behind, even though he knew in his heart it was the right thing to do. There was no doubt in his mind that Duncan would protect Olivia, the baby and Aaron with his life.

He prayed such a sacrifice wouldn't be necessary.

Keeping his attention focused on the road, he followed the directions to Seth's home. He'd memorized the location by looking at the map he'd pulled up on the computer in the motel, while Olivia had been in the bathroom.

Thinking of Olivia brought a new surge of guilt. She was becoming far too dependent on him, and that wasn't good.

The fact that he was just as emotionally involved with her didn't help. This brief time apart would be good for both of them.

He made sure there were no signs of the mercenaries as he drove toward Madison. The closer he got to the capital city of Wisconsin, the harder it was to figure out if anyone was on his tail.

Seth's address was in Sun Prairie, which was on the other side of the city. The traffic was crazy busy, often bumper-to-bumper, as he made his way around the city, bypassing the congested downtown area, toward the suburbs.

Finally, he found Bakerville Street and drove past without stopping, taking a quick survey of the neighborhood. It was quiet, without a lot of people around, indicating many of the home-owners might be at work.

After making a large loop around the subdivision, he parked on the street that ran behind Bakerville. On foot, he went through a yard that was overgrown with weeds, then crouched behind a bush to watch the rear of Seth's house.

There wasn't any hint of activity within the house or in the surrounding area. Had he come too early? It was the middle of the afternoon, and for all he knew, Seth was one of the mercenaries that had been sent after Olivia.

The thought was depressing. Still, he didn't move for a full five minutes. Finally, he retreated, after deciding he'd need to return after dark. If Willis wasn't home then, he'd search the place for any potential clues.

After he was back in the SUV and driving away, Ryker realized he'd jumped on the chance to leave the motel, without considering the possibility that Seth wasn't home.

Idiot. That was what happened when you let a woman mess with your concentration.

Ten minutes outside of Sun Prairie, he pulled into a parking lot and called Duncan.

"Find him?"

"Not yet. Place looks deserted." He wondered if Duncan thought he was an idiot, too. "Looks like I'll need to stick around until later tonight, to go in under the cover of darkness."

Duncan remained silent, no doubt questioning Ryker's judgment. "Well, you should come back here, then. Better to work together to come up with a plan."

Because he liked the idea of returning far too much, he rejected it. "No, traffic through the city was ridiculous. Besides, I want to keep an eye on the place. If Willis shows, I'll go in and talk to him. I just wanted you to know this will take longer than planned."

"And you want me to tell Olivia you'll be delayed indefinitely."

"Yes." He inwardly winced. "I'm sorry, Dunc. I know she won't be happy."

"We'll be fine. I'll pick them up something for dinner."

His gut clenched. "Don't leave them alone. Take them with you."

"Telling me how to do my job, Tillman?" Thankfully, there was a note of wry humor in his tone. "I think I can handle it."

"Yeah. Sure. I'll be in touch." Ryker disconnected before he could make a bigger mess of things.

It had been a long time since he'd done any stakeout work. After leaving the army, he'd done private bodyguard work for a while, then opened his own security business. Different from what the Blake-Moore Group did, Ryker's job was to enhance the safety measures for private companies.

Not take out anyone perceived to be a threat.

After doing a little more recon, Ryker decided to buy a pair of binoculars and hide out in the tree house located catty-corner from Seth's house.

An hour later, he was safely settled in the tree house, savoring the partially obstructed view of Seth's driveway and front door. The garage was out of sight, but if a car pulled into the drive, he'd see it.

Ignoring the discomfort, he watched and waited. Being here like this reminded him of his tour in Afghanistan. The temperature was unseasonably cool for June, which was better than the heat and dust he'd experienced overseas.

Activity in the neighborhood picked up around dinnertime as residents returned home after a long day of work. He was about to give up on Seth ever returning home, when he finally caught a glimpse of a dark blue car pulling into the driveway.

He sharpened the scopes on the binocs and felt a surge of satisfaction when he recognized Seth's face behind the wheel. The guy glanced nervously over his shoulder, as if sensing Ryker's gaze, before the car rolled out of sight, presumably into the garage.

Ryker watched for several minutes, hoping to catch a glimpse of Seth through the living room window. But the windows were all covered with blinds in a way that indicated Seth was taking precautions to remain hidden.

Because he was in trouble with the Blake-Moore Group? Or because it was second nature to him, the way it was to any soldier who'd seen combat?

There was no way of knowing for sure, but he hoped there was a way to convince Seth to cooperate once he had him alone.

Which might prove to be a problem. Seth was bunkered down in the house and Ryker didn't exactly relish breaking in.

He sat back against the rough-hewn boards of the tree house. How could he get Seth to come out of the house? He snapped his fingers as an idea came to him.

A diversion.

Digging into the front pocket of his black jeans, he pulled out a lighter. He'd never smoked but had learned that they were handy devices when you needed to start a fire in the woods.

Or, in this case, a small fire to draw Seth out of the house.

The minutes dragged by slowly, turning into one hour, then two. By seven o'clock, the normal brightness was dimmed by the dark clouds accumulating overhead. Thanks to the impending storm, he was able to make his move earlier than planned.

After leaving the tree house, he made his way to the garbage and recycling bins sitting curbside a few doors down. Rummaging in the recycle bin provided him with discarded newspaper.

Moving slowly and quietly, he once again went through the unkempt yard to the rear of Seth's house. Crouching behind the bush, he could see a tiny bit of light around the blinds of the kitchen window.

He looked for a vent that might lead inside. A dryer vent, maybe? There wasn't one anywhere in sight. After agonizing for several minutes, he made a quick dash to the back door.

There was a screen door covering the interior one. Twisting the handle, he found it wasn't locked, although the inside one was.

He found a large rock and used it to prop open the screen door. Then he balled the newspaper and set it on fire.

Stepping back from the door, he pressed himself against the side of the house and waited. The scent of smoke was strong, but he couldn't be sure any of it was actually getting inside.

But his patience was rewarded when the door abruptly opened. "What in the world—"

Ryker jumped over the burning paper, which was quickly becoming nothing but ashes, forcing Seth backward into the house.

Having been caught off guard, Seth tried to fight. He swung at Ryker, but Ryker slid to the side and grabbed Seth's arm, pulling him off-balance. They tumbled to the floor, Seth continuing to struggle. But Ryker had a position of strength, not to mention sheer determination. He had to find out what the Blake-Moore Group wanted with Olivia.

Finally, he had Seth pinned to the floor. "Tell me what I need to know and you'll live to see another day."

Seth glared up at him, his mouth pulled into a grim line. He didn't say a word, which wasn't unexpected.

Each of the mercenaries he'd come up against so far had been the exact same way. Too well trained to talk, to rat out their comrades. Unless they happened to be semiconscious.

Ryker was tired of the act.

Thunder boomed overhead and within moments rain began to fall. He was glad to know the fire he'd started would be out soon.

"You won't talk? Fine, just listen. I was one of the men who helped take down Tim Habush and Colin Yonkers. You want to be next? Fine with me. But you should know that we're onto Kevin Blake and Harper Moore. They're not going to win this thing, do you understand? We will not stop until we take them down."

Still nothing. With an abrupt move, Seth tried to twist out of Ryker's grip, but he'd been expecting it, and managed to stay on top, tightening the pressure.

"There's an innocent pregnant woman and child in the middle of this mess. Do you really want to be responsible for their deaths? A pregnant woman and her baby? A three-year-old boy?"

Something flared in Seth's eyes and Ryker felt certain the news of Olivia's pregnancy had caught the guy off guard.

Good. He needed something, anything to convince the man to talk.

"Why are mercenaries from Blake-Moore coming after Olivia Habush?"

No response.

"What possible threat could a pregnant woman be to their organization?"

Still nothing, but again the flicker in Seth's

eyes betrayed the fact that Tim's cousin hadn't known about the baby.

Maybe there was at least one line the mercenary wouldn't cross.

"I have all night, Willis. I'm not leaving until I get what I want."

Seth glanced away, focusing on some spot behind Ryker's ear. He hoped and prayed the slight movement meant the guy's resistance was weakening.

He really didn't want to be here all night.

"Are you worried about Blake-Moore seeking retaliation against you? I can help you get away from them. I happen to be on a first-name basis with Senator Rick Barton and he has friends in the FBI. I'm sure we can arrange protection."

Seth's eyes met his briefly, then slid away, staring blindly at the same spot behind his ear.

"It's your funeral." Ryker lowered his voice in a tone that he hoped sounded threatening. "It's one thing to die serving our country, but do you really want to die for Blake-Moore? What have they done for you?"

Another long silence, but the way Seth's mouth tightened made him think he was finally getting through.

"You're not the first to die over this." He hadn't intended to kill anyone, but Seth didn't need to know that. "I took out the first two mercenaries who came after Olivia, then took care of two more. How many others does Blake-Moore have in their back pocket? You're disposable, Willis. They don't care about you. All they want is Olivia. When you're dead, they'll easily find a replacement." He leaned down, getting into Seth's face. "They won't miss you when you're gone."

Seth's expression remained stoic but Ryker felt certain his words were getting under Seth's skin. What he'd said about the Blake-Moore Group was true. They wouldn't care one bit if Seth died here tonight.

"Numbers."

The word was so unexpectedly familiar, he wondered if he'd imagined it. "Numbers? Blake-Moore is looking for numbers?"

"Yeah."

Ryker waited for him to elaborate. "I need more, Seth. Why is Olivia involved? Do they think she has these numbers? And what are they related to?"

"I want protection."

Ryker wondered if this was a trap. If the minute he let up on the pressure, Seth would fight to get away. "I can get Senator Barton and the FBI to provide protection. If you cooperate with me. But so far, you've given me squat."

"Bank accounts." Seth's body relaxed beneath

his, but Ryker didn't let up. "Tim and Colin were skimming from the company."

That was an angle he hadn't considered. At the same time, it wasn't a complete surprise. Men who would threaten to kill innocent women and children would just as easily steal from their employer.

"They think Olivia has access to the bank accounts?" He remembered the receipts in Olivia's house.

"I don't know. I walked away after Tim and Colin died. Decided I wasn't going to put my life on the line for Blake-Moore." His tone was bitter. "I work as a hospital security guard now. The money isn't great, but I'm dating a nurse, which is better than getting shot at."

It was. "I'm going to let you up. But if you try anything, you'll never get the protection you need."

Seth nodded, his gaze weary. Ryker surged to his feet. He checked the fire he'd started, made sure any lingering flames were out, then rattled off the personal phone number for Senator Rick Barton. Seth scrambled for a piece of paper and a pen, taking notes.

Ryker now had the information he'd come for, but it wasn't very helpful. Olivia hadn't known about her husband's embezzling.

Had she?

He strode toward the doorway, determined to find out.

ELEVEN

On a whim, Ryker decided to stop at Olivia and Tim's house prior to heading back to the motel. Logically, he didn't think there would be additional clues to uncover. Certainly someone from Blake-Moore would have already checked out the place, but he figured it was worth a shot.

And it wouldn't take too long.

Remembering the stack of receipts he'd found back in December made him think there was a slim possibility that there may be something valuable buried in there. Were they all just receipts for household items? Or was there something important hidden in plain sight?

The place looked even more forlorn and neglected than before. It occurred to him that once the danger was over, Olivia and Aaron would have a home to return to. The house was hers, if she could continue making the payments.

Which made him wonder if the bank was on

the brink of foreclosing on the property already. For her sake, he hoped not.

The back door was still unlocked, the way it had been six months ago. As he entered, the sour milk smell hit hard, worse than before, and intermingled with other rotten food likely from the fridge. The interior looked just as bad as last time he'd been there, but not much worse. Blake-Moore had evidently tried to cover their tracks, leaving no obvious signs behind.

He found the receipts in the kitchen, appearing untouched from his last visit. Quickly reviewing a few of them didn't reveal anything interesting, but he swept them into a pile to take back to the motel anyway. It wouldn't hurt to go through them one by one.

Scanning the interior of the house, he tried to think about where proof of the bank accounts may be. Was there a ledger stashed somewhere? Or some other place where bank-account numbers were written down? If there was, the men Blake-Moore had sent should have found them, but maybe they hadn't looked hard enough.

He could only hope they'd missed something.

He worked his way methodically through the house, feeling a bit like he was invading Olivia's privacy, especially when it came to searching the master bedroom. Yet he didn't find anything remotely related to bank-account information.

Just as he was about to leave, he hesitated, then decided he should pack a bag for Olivia, knowing she'd love fresh clothes to wear.

At least the trip here wouldn't be a total waste of time.

When he'd finished packing some of Olivia's and Aaron's things, he searched Aaron's room. A child's bedroom would be a great hiding spot. He lifted the mattress off the small bed, and searched the box of Pull-Ups that had been left behind, along with the dresser drawers and closet.

Nothing.

Dejected, he returned to the kitchen, grabbed the receipts and stuffed them into an empty envelope. After placing the envelope in the overnight bag, he swung it over his shoulder and left the house the way he'd come. As he made his way back to his vehicle, he decided to ask Olivia about the mortgage payments. If she wanted a place to return to once the danger was over, he could help make the house payments until things had settled down.

Even if she didn't want to live here anymore, she could still sell the place, then use the money to start over somewhere new.

Near him?

Yeah, right. He pushed the ridiculous idea aside. No doubt, once Olivia and Aaron were safe, and her baby was born, she wouldn't want anything to do with him.

Except she *had* kissed him.

A rash decision in the heat of the moment. He'd been her sole protector and she probably hadn't been thinking clearly. Best not to remember how much he'd enjoyed her kiss.

He focused his attention on driving back to Cambridge, making sure he didn't pick up a tail.

When he arrived at the motel, he found Duncan pacing in agitation, like a caged wild animal. Duncan rushed over when he walked in, putting Ryker instantly on alert. "What happened? What's wrong?"

"Olivia's having labor pains."

"What?" Panic washed over him, and he hurried through the connecting door to her room. He found her seated upright on the bed, her back resting against the headboard. She looked calm as she smoothed her hands over her rounded stomach. "Are you okay? Do we need to go to the hospital?"

"I'm fine." Her smile was strained. "These aren't real labor pains, just Braxton-Hicks."

"Braxton who?" He wanted to do something, anything to make sure she didn't go into early labor. "We should at least have a doctor look at you."

"Relax, Ryker. I had these with Aaron, too."

Some of the tension left his shoulders, but not much. He'd never felt more helpless than he did at this moment. He didn't care what she experienced before, being on the run these past few days had been stressful.

And stress wasn't good for Olivia or the baby.

He wasn't a total stranger to God and faith, after all; he knew Hawk and Jillian were churchgoers. Still, he hadn't thought much of it for himself, until recently. He'd never known his father, and his mother had abandoned him when he was young, leaving him a ward of the state. He'd eventually found a home with a nice couple, but he had moved around frequently for several years before that happened.

It wasn't until he'd started hanging around the Callahans and now Hawk, that he'd learned about church and faith. At first he hadn't understood why it was such a big deal, but now with Olivia and Aaron depending on him, he liked the idea of God watching over them.

He was prepared to do whatever was necessary to keep Olivia safe, but he had never anticipated she might go into labor. He had no idea how to deliver a baby!

Another swell of panic rose within him, nearly choking him.

He found himself sending up a quick prayer on their behalf.

Please, Lord, keep Olivia from delivering her baby early. Keep her, Aaron and her baby safe!

Olivia really wasn't worried about the Braxton-Hicks, but the stark fear on Ryker's face gave her pause. For the first time since he'd rescued her from the men in the Blake-Moore Group, he looked as if he might throw up.

That was her role to play, not his. She closed her eyes and concentrated on slow, deep breathing. The contractions weren't regular or strong, which were both good signs. And they were very similar to the Braxton-Hicks contractions she'd experienced with Aaron.

Still, she'd prayed hard over the past thirty minutes, asking for God's grace and mercy in watching over her unborn child. Thankfully, Aaron had remained preoccupied with his television show, oblivious to what she was experiencing.

"Olivia?" Ryker's low voice sent shivers of awareness skating down her spine. She really, really needed to get a grip on her hormones.

"I'm fine, Ryker." She opened her eyes and offered a faint smile. "I think the contractions have stopped."

"Good." Ryker hesitated for a moment, before taking a seat on the edge of the bed beside her, his expression serious. "I don't want you to wait too long. You need to tell me when we need to go to the hospital, all right?"

"I will." She wasn't going to take any chances on having a premature baby. Aaron had been a week late, so she hadn't been expecting a problem with this pregnancy. "You were gone a long time. How did it go with Seth? Did you find him? Talk to him?"

"Yeah. I convinced him to talk." His brow furrowed. "I don't want to add any more stress, Olivia, but I need to ask you about the bank accounts."

She looked at him blankly. "What bank accounts?"

"Seth mentioned bank accounts. He seems to think they're the reason Blake-Moore is coming after you." His hazel gaze searched hers. "You really don't know anything about them?"

"Tim and I have a joint bank account, or at least we did. I didn't dare use or access it since the first few days after leaving the motel."

"I don't mean to intrude on your personal business, but how much money is in there?"

She didn't understand where he was going with this line of questioning. "Maybe six or seven thousand dollars? Tim made good money, and we didn't spend above our means." In fact, she'd preferred shopping for bargains, especially once she'd learned she was pregnant.

"Do you think that money has been going toward your mortgage payments?"

"Yes. The bank takes the money automatically from our account each month." She hadn't really thought of it until now. "Although if that's the case, I think the money will run out very shortly if it hasn't already." She blew out a heavy breath. "I hate the thought of the bank foreclosing on the house."

"I don't want you to worry about it." Ryker put a reassuring hand on her arm. "I'll take care of everything."

"You can't pay my mortgage." She was horrified at the offer. "I'm sure this will be over soon. I doubt the bank will foreclose until I miss several payments." At least, she hoped not.

"Don't stress. It will be fine."

The idea of going back to the house she'd shared with Tim filled her with distaste. No way. She wouldn't do it. But she could sell the property. Yes, that was the answer. She'd sell and move back to the small town of Harrisburg. Except… Willa wouldn't be there. Remembering how Willa had died helping to protect Aaron made her grimace.

Far better to find somewhere else to live. Somewhere just like Harrisburg. A smaller community where neighbors knew each other and watched out for each other.

Where she could find a wonderfully welcoming church like the one Willa had taken her to in Harrisburg.

"What about these receipts?"

Ryker's voice pulled her attention back to the issue at hand. She looked down at the envelope of receipts he'd spread out on the bed. "Where did you get these?"

"Your house."

Her gaze collided with his. "You went back there?"

He nodded. "I brought a bag back with some clean clothes for you and Aaron." He cleared his throat as if embarrassed. "I hope you don't mind."

"Normally I would, but I'm so desperate to get out of these old things, I'll gladly take whatever you brought for us, as long as they fit me. Thank you." She dropped her gaze to the receipts and picked one off the top. "These are just household items I purchased. Groceries, toiletries." She picked up another, feeling despondent over the loss of the life she once had. Not that she necessarily missed the man Tim had become, but still, living from day to day in relative safety had been nice. Something she'd never again take for granted. "A discount store where I purchased items for Aaron." Her gaze met his. "Why did you bring these here?"

"I'm not sure. I just thought they might be helpful." He held her gaze, then added, "You need to know that Seth informed me Tim and Colin were stealing money from the Blake-Moore Group."

"What?" She didn't think she could be shocked at anything Tim had done, but the news was startling. "Are you sure?"

He lifted a shoulder. "According to Seth, they'd been at it for a while. I take it you didn't know anything about it."

"No." She felt light-headed, the blood leaving her face in a rush, and was grateful she was already sitting down. "Why would they do such a thing? Tim made good money, enough that he encouraged me to quit my part-time job as an accountant."

"I don't know." His eyes were filled with empathy. "Greed often has no limit."

"Greed." She let out a harsh laugh. "I guess that sums it up right there. Tim always wanted more, felt he deserved more, but Colin…" She shook her head unable to finish. "I hate knowing how Tim dragged my brother down with him."

"Tell me about the morning you left the house."

The change in subject made her sigh. "That

was months ago. What good will it do to go over it all again?"

"Please, humor me."

She blew out a frustrated breath, thinking back to that morning just before Christmas. She'd started the day full of hope, thinking that maybe once Tim learned she was pregnant, he'd change. That he'd go back to the way things used to be.

Although based on what she'd just learned, she knew that things would never have changed. Except for the worse.

"Colin and Jeff came into the kitchen as Aaron and I were eating breakfast."

"Did he have a key?" Ryker asked.

"My brother did, yes. Not Jeff." She waved an impatient hand. "Anyway, Colin told me that we were all in danger and that we had to leave immediately."

"But he didn't say what the danger was?"

"No." She gave him an exasperated look. "Are you going to keep interrupting me or are you going to let me tell the story?"

"Sorry." Ryker looked chagrined. "Tell the story."

She thought back. "I asked Colin what was going on, even as I washed Aaron's face and hands from his breakfast. Colin told me he didn't have time to explain, because we had to move in a hurry. I asked if I could pack a bag for both of us, since it sounded like we'd be gone for at least a couple of days, but Colin said there was no time."

When she paused, Ryker asked, "So then what?"

"I told Colin we needed Aaron's car seat, so he sent Jeff out to grab it. Then as I carried Aaron to the door, Colin told me to make sure I took Aaron's diaper bag."

Ryker's eyebrows levered upward. "He actually said that? To take the diaper bag?"

She nodded. "I figured he mentioned it specifically because of the car seat. Like I should take some important things, but not worry about clothes and toiletries."

She followed Ryker's gaze as he turned and looked at the zebra-striped diaper bag. "We need to empty that thing."

A wave of frustration hit her hard. "Come on, Ryker. I've been using that bag on and off for the past six months. Don't you think I would have noticed if there was some sort of notebook full of bank-account information hidden inside?"

"Probably." Ryker leaned over and grabbed the bag. "But it can't hurt to check again."

He set the bag on her lap, and she took out the Pull-Ups diapers first and set them aside.

Then she pulled out a change of clothing she always carried for Aaron and set the outfit on top of the diapers.

"Hold on." Ryker reached for the clothes. She watched as he quickly went over the seams of the clothing. When he finished, he noticed her gaze and shrugged. "Hey, it doesn't hurt to check."

"You want to go through the container of wipes, too?" She pulled that out next.

"No, thanks. You made your point."

She pulled out her wallet and handed it over. "You should probably check this. I've used the cash I'd managed to smuggle away from Jeff, but none of the credit cards."

He peered into every pocket and card slot of her wallet, then handed it back. "Nothing."

It didn't take long for her to empty the rest of the bag. "I told you—there's nothing here." She sat back against the headboard, suddenly exhausted.

The Blake-Moore Group continued to come after her because of the money. Everything came down to pure greed.

Maybe if she could find a way to explain to them that she didn't have their stupid numbers, they'd leave her and Aaron alone.

Maybe.

"Let me see the bag." Ryker lifted it off her

lap and began running his fingers along the seams. She wondered if the stress was getting to him, too, because he wasn't exactly behaving normally.

But then he pulled out the cardboard covered in plastic at the bottom of the diaper bag. Liv frowned as he turned it over in his hands.

"There's a slit along the side." He used the tip of his fingernail to lift the edge of the plastic up from the cardboard.

A slip of paper floated out, landing on her legs.

For a moment they both stared at it, in shocked surprise. Ryker reached it first, then met her gaze.

"The bank-account information has been in the diaper bag all along." He showed her the small printed rows of account numbers with corresponding deposits. Her breath caught when she took note of the total.

Just over five million.

She couldn't believe it. Nausea swirled and she swallowed hard. "I don't understand. Why would Colin hide this in the diaper bag?"

"I don't know, unless Tim told him to do it. After all, Colin is the one who took you to the motel. Could be that Tim hoped to finish the job with Hawk and then get out of town before accessing the money."

Her shoulders slumped in defeat. More evidence of how far gone her brother and husband had been.

And their greed had put her and Aaron right in the bull's-eye of danger.

TWELVE

Setting aside the slip of paper he'd found hiding in the bottom of the zebra bag, he slid over along the edge of the bed and placed his arm around Olivia's thin shoulders. She looked pale and wan, as if she might pass out at any moment.

"It's okay." He tried to sound reassuring even though he knew this new evidence wasn't going to make things any better for them. Finding the information was one thing. Figuring out the next step in bringing down the Blake-Moore Group was something else.

"It's not," she whispered. He felt her draw in a deep breath and rest her head against his shoulder. "Tim and Colin are dead, and for what? Money?"

Five million was a life-changing amount of cash, but frankly, he didn't get it, either. Especially because Olivia had claimed the Blake-Moore Group paid her husband a decent salary.

He rubbed his hand up and down her arm. "I'm sorry they dragged you and your son into this."

She sniffled and he felt awful knowing she was crying. "He never loved me or Aaron."

He couldn't find the words to argue, because her late husband's actions spoke for themselves. No man should ever put his wife and son in danger the way Tim Habush had. No man should sacrifice his entire family for the contents of a bank account. Five million was nothing compared to a wife and child, especially considering the guy hadn't lived long enough to spend a dime.

He couldn't understand why Tim had thrown away the precious gift of his family, but Ryker was very glad to be with Olivia now. And he was more determined than ever to keep all of them—Olivia, her baby and Aaron—safe.

Duncan poked his head through the connecting door. When he saw Olivia in Ryker's arms, his brow raised and he flashed a knowing grin, then quickly disappeared.

"I wish Tim had been more like you, Ryker."

Her statement caught him off guard, and an unexpected flash of longing hit hard. His feelings for Olivia and Aaron were getting out of control. He cared about her, about them, far too much.

He tried to remind himself about how he'd

gone down the path of having a family with Cheri and Cyndi. How they'd been killed before he'd had a chance to know what having a real family of his own would be like. Growing up in the foster-care system, he'd dreamed of having a family. But since losing Cheri and Cyndi, he had no interest in trying again.

Last Christmas he'd silently promised to find Olivia and her son, in order to help keep them safe. The way he wished someone had helped Cheri and her little girl.

After finding Olivia, he'd learned to admire her strength and courage. Her sweetness when she talked about her baby. She was everything he'd once liked about Cheri, only more.

Unable to think of a coherent response, Ryker bent down to press a kiss to her temple.

Olivia shifted in his arms, tipping her head back to look up at him. For a long moment their gazes clung, her eyes searching his. His throat seemed to have stopped working, along with his brain, since he couldn't think of anything to say.

She reached up and cradled his cheek with her palm. "You are a wonderful man, Ryker. I'm so blessed God sent you to come and find me."

Her gratitude battered the wall he'd built around his heart, knocking several bricks loose. He dropped his gaze to her lush mouth. Before he could blink, she drew his head down so she could kiss him.

Their lips clung, then melded together in a heart-stopping caress. Her sweet taste made him long for more.

Not just having her in his arms, which he absolutely wanted, but having her, Aaron and the baby in his life.

The thought brought him up short. Olivia must have noticed, because she broke off the kiss.

"Sorry, I don't know what's wrong with me." She looked adorably flustered, but he didn't like the self-recrimination in her eyes.

He finally found his voice. "There is absolutely nothing wrong with you, Olivia."

She grimaced. "Except that I keep kissing a man who has been nothing but kind to me."

He threaded his fingers through her chin-length dark hair. "I've imagined kissing you several times. You've just been brave enough to take action."

"Yeah, right." She rested her hand on her belly. "I highly doubt there's a man out there who dreams of kissing a pregnant woman who resembles a baby whale."

He placed his hand over hers. "You're beautiful, Olivia. Don't sell yourself short. But you need to know that being in danger like this heightens emotions that wouldn't normally develop on their own."

She frowned. "Duncan put his life on the line for me, but I don't feel this way toward him."

He was ridiculously pleased at her assertion, but knew she was oversimplifying the situation. "But I was the one who found you first. If the situation was reversed, and it was Duncan who came after you, I think you'd be sitting here right now with him."

"No." The stubborn glint was back in her eyes, and he was a bit relieved that she seemed to have momentarily forgotten about the bank-account numbers that had sent the Blake-Moore mercenaries gunning for her. "I wouldn't."

He didn't believe her, and decided it was time to change the subject. "We can talk more about this once you and Aaron are safe. For now, I need some time to discuss our next steps with Duncan."

"I want to give the bank information over to the Blake-Moore Group. Once they have what they've wanted all along, they'll leave me and Aaron alone."

He went still. "We can't do that."

Her gaze narrowed. "Why not? The money belongs to them, doesn't it? Tim and Colin stole from the company. It's only fair they get it back."

Ryker blew out a frustrated breath. "It's blood money. Men have died because of it. And it's highly likely that the money is what they received from dealing weapons to the enemy."

"We don't know that." She pulled her hand out from beneath his and edged away. "Don't you understand? I just want this to be over. I want to live my life with Aaron and have my baby without worrying about someone coming after us."

He didn't want to scare her, but there was no way in the world it would be as easy as handing over the banking information. "They're not just going to let you walk away, Olivia. Or me, for that matter."

A hint of worry flashed in her eyes. "The money is likely more important than revenge."

"And what's to stop us from going to the police to tell them what the Blake-Moore Group has done?"

"We'll give them our word that we won't." A thread of doubt underlined her tone, as if she was finally beginning to understand the magnitude of the danger they still faced.

Ryker rose to his feet and picked up the account numbers. "Give me some time to talk this over with Duncan, okay? Maybe we can come up with a couple of options."

She hesitated, then nodded. "Fine, but think

about all the options we have available to us. Sometimes easier is better."

Ryker smiled. "I will. Now do me a favor and get some rest."

"I will."

Every cell in his body wanted to draw her into his arms again, to kiss her until they both couldn't breathe, but he forced himself to take one step, then another toward the connecting door.

"Good night, Ryker."

Her soft voice gave him pause, and he glanced over his shoulder. "Good night, Olivia."

Leaving the connecting door open about an inch, he listened as she and Aaron prepared to go to sleep.

This was the wrong place and the wrong time for him to fall for another single mother. He knew that Olivia's feelings were intermingled with hero worship after the way he'd come to her rescue.

But his weren't. They were all too real, and frankly, they scared him to death.

More than the Blake-Moore Group did.

The next morning, Olivia woke early, after having one of the best night's sleep she'd had since this nightmare had started.

Because of Ryker and Duncan watching over her, she felt safer than she had in a long time.

A shower and change of clothes felt wonderful, even if it was a bit embarrassing to know Ryker had gone through her things.

After she'd changed her son, she took Aaron's hand and walked to the connecting door that was hanging ajar. She lightly rapped on the door frame. "Ryker? Duncan?"

The door opened almost immediately. Ryker's smile made her knees go weak and she hoped she wasn't blushing. "Hey, how did you sleep?"

"Great." He opened the door wide, giving her and Aaron room to come inside. She nodded toward Duncan who was seated at a small desk with an open laptop computer before him. "Did you guys get any rest?"

"Sure." Duncan's brief grin made her wonder if he was glossing over how much they'd slept. "Take a seat. We have a plan we'd like to discuss."

"A plan?" She glanced at Ryker. His hazel stare was steady and she had the feeling that no matter what she thought about it, their plan was already a go. "I thought you were going to come up with a few options?"

"Just listen first, okay?" Ryker's tone was gentle. "And please sit down."

"Standing isn't going to make me go into

labor." She inwardly winced at her cranky tone. Why was she annoyed? After all, she'd slept well and so had Aaron. She set him up with cartoons on the television, then eased down onto the edge of the bed. "Okay, tell me your plan."

The two men exchanged a glance, then Ryker pulled up a chair so that he was eye level with her.

"Remember how I mentioned the Callahans all work in law enforcement?"

"Yes. They're a large family, and all their names start with the letter *M*." She'd thought that hilarious and wondered how many times their parents had called the wrong kid by the wrong name.

"That's right. The oldest, Marc Callahan, works for the FBI."

Oh yes, she remembered that. She straightened and glanced at Duncan, before meeting Ryker's gaze. Then it hit her. "You think the FBI is interested in the guns being sold to the enemy."

"Yes, we do. And it's not just that, but Hawk became acquainted with an FBI agent while he was trying to find who was behind the attempts to kill him and his family."

"Special Agent in Charge Dennis Ludwig," Duncan added. "We think it's a good idea to reach out to Marc Callahan and explain what's going on. Marc can be our liaison with Ludwig."

"Why not give Blake-Moore the account numbers?" She knew she sounded like a broken record, but it seemed very logical to her. Give them what they wanted in exchange for being left alone. "With five million they could likely disappear forever."

"And what would stop them from killing us all?" Again, Ryker's tone was gentle. "No witnesses to ever come forward against them."

She reached up to rub her temple. The feeling of being well rested was fading fast beneath the harsh reality Ryker and Duncan were presenting. "We aren't witnesses to anything."

"We know the bank accounts that house the money that was siphoned away by your husband and brother." Ryker hesitated, then added, "And don't forget, two of their men died by our hands, three others assaulted and tied up. Don't you see? We absolutely need to bring the authorities in on this."

She sighed and nodded, admitting defeat. "You're right. Okay, we'll bring in the authorities. But how long will it take for the FBI to arrest Harper Moore and Kevin Blake? Days? Weeks? Months? A year?"

The two men exchanged another knowing

glance. "We don't know," Duncan admitted. "But hopefully not longer than a few months."

She placed a protective hand on her stomach. "We don't have a few months. This baby is due in just under six weeks. A little less, now."

"I know. Don't worry, Olivia. It's going to be okay." Ryker put a reassuring hand on her arm. "We're going to protect you, Aaron and the baby. I'm sure the FBI will help us."

She should be relieved to know that the FBI would be helping to protect her, but she wasn't. The idea of having a couple of straitlaced FBI agents dressed in suits and ties watching over her was not reassuring. While he might be a perfectly nice guy, she didn't know or have a reason to trust Dennis Ludwig or any other FBI agent.

She wanted Ryker. Yet for the first time, it occurred to her that maybe he was tired of being in the line of fire on her behalf. After all, he'd done more than his fair share of fighting off the bad guys since he'd found her in Harrisburg.

Her cheeks burned at the memory of how she'd kissed him. Twice. Why on earth had she done that? Based on the fact that he'd tried to convince her that her emotions were some form of hero worship made her realize just how one-sided they were.

The way he'd been kind enough to tell her she

was beautiful, when she was as big as a house, was sweet. His way of trying to soften the blow.

He didn't want her or care about her the way she was beginning to care about him. This plan of going to the FBI for help was obviously two-fold.

Get the feds involved in bringing down Harper Moore and Kevin Blake, while extricating himself from her life.

Okay, then. She straightened her shoulders. "All right."

A momentary confusion washed over Ryker's face. "All right, what? You're in agreement with us reaching out to Marc Callahan?"

"Yes. And to bringing in the FBI, that agent in charge." She searched for his name. "Dennis Ludwig."

"Great." Duncan pounced on her agreement. "I'll call Marc now. He should be back in Milwaukee by now."

Ryker looked as if he wanted to say something more, but Aaron's plaintive tone interrupted them.

"Mommy, I'm hungry."

She turned away from Ryker. "Okay, sweetie. I'll get you some animal crackers."

Ryker jumped up and crossed through the connecting doors to get her zebra bag. She stared at it for a moment, hating the idea that she'd been carrying the stupid bank-account numbers in there all this time, then told herself not to be foolish.

The bag wasn't the problem, the numbers were.

"Duncan, see if Marc can meet us for breakfast," Ryker said. "We'll meet him halfway if necessary."

Duncan raised a hand to acknowledge him, but remained focused on his call. "Marc? Hey, it's Duncan O'Hare. Do you have a minute? We have a bit of a problem…"

Duncan left the motel room, talking to Marc as he went. She wasn't sure why he needed privacy. She knew everything that had gone down, but decided it was better for Aaron not to hear any of the specifics.

Her son was satisfied with a couple of animal crackers, his gaze locked on the television.

She second-guessed her decision several times over the next twenty minutes. Marc had agreed to meet with them in about an hour, so Ryker had advised her to pack up their things.

"We won't be back."

"But won't it take time for Marc to get in touch with Dennis Ludwig?"

Ryker nodded. "We'll still find somewhere else to stay. Better to keep moving."

"All right." It didn't take long for her to gather their things, stuffing everything into the zebra bag.

Thirty minutes later they were on the road. This time Duncan was tucked in the back seat beside Aaron. He was great with her son, keeping him entertained by reciting stories that he must have memorized from children's books.

"How does he know so many of them?" she asked Ryker.

"He spends a lot of time with his nephew Brodie."

She remembered hearing about Mike Callahan and Shayla's son. "He must have a really good memory."

"Nah. I've just read the books about a hundred times each," Duncan said in a wry tone. "I could recite them in my sleep."

The family restaurant wasn't too far off the interstate. They chose a circular booth that offered room for four seats and a high chair for Aaron.

Her stomach rumbled at the enticing scent of bacon and eggs. Ryker must have heard, as he grinned. "Let's order."

"I'll be fine. We can wait for Marc," she protested.

"Marc is running a bit late," Duncan said with a glance at his phone. "He said to go ahead and order. He'll eat on the way."

Their meal arrived in what seemed like record time. She dove into her over-easy eggs, then realized she forgot to pray, so sent up a quick, silent *Thank You, Lord* before continuing to eat.

Based on the liberal smears of syrup over his face, Aaron was enjoying his French toast.

She glanced longingly at the coffee Ryker and Duncan were drinking, but told herself to forget it. She remained determined to avoid anything that may impact the baby. Sipping her water, she watched as the two men quickly devoured their meals.

Pushing her empty plate away, she sighed. "That was good, thanks. Please excuse me for a moment." She slid out of the booth intending to use the restroom.

Ryker's hand clamped on her arm. "Wait. Duncan, do you see that SUV that just pulled in? Notice the dark tinted windows? Just like the other SUV Blake-Moore used?"

"Yeah." He lifted his phone to his ear. "Marc? We've got company."

SUV? Company? Her heart squeezed in her chest. No, this couldn't be happening again. Could it?

How was it possible that the Blake-Moore Group had found them again?

THIRTEEN

"We're getting out of here." Ryker wasn't about to take any chances. He tossed cash on the table, lifted Aaron out of his high chair, grabbed the zebra bag and placed his hand in the small of Olivia's back, steering her toward the opposite end of the restaurant. Duncan followed, still talking to Marc.

"I don't understand..." Olivia began.

"Not now." He didn't mean to sound terse, but this wasn't the time for a detailed conversation. "Go through the kitchen."

"The kitchen?" Olivia's voice rose in agitation. "They won't let us in."

He ignored her, since he wasn't planning to ask permission, and pushed the swinging door open with one hand. With the other, he gently nudged her through.

"Hey!" The kitchen help gaped at them. "Customers aren't allowed back here."

"Don't worry, we're just moving through."

Ryker raked his gaze over the area, searching for the back door that he knew all restaurants had for employee use. When he saw the dark green door, he urged Olivia toward it.

He half expected someone to physically attempt to stop them, but they didn't. Instead, the staff stayed where they were, as if momentarily frozen in time, watching them. Thirty seconds later, they were outside near a large Dumpster, with an open field behind it.

The lack of coverage made him nervous.

"Where's Marc?" He glanced toward Duncan. "We need an escape strategy."

"I know." Duncan still had his phone to his ear. "He's coming up now."

"I see him." A silver SUV came around the corner, with a dark-haired man behind the wheel. Ryker had met the entire Callahan family several times, but it wasn't always easy to tell them apart. Marc was the oldest and most serious of the bunch. Although he was a different man when he was around his wife, Kari, and his two young children.

"Wait. I need a car seat for Aaron." Olivia dug in her heels in protest when he urged her toward the SUV.

"Marc has kids, too," Duncan assured her. "See? There's a car seat in the back."

That was all Olivia needed. She rushed forward, opening the back passenger door. She reached for her son, but Ryker was already setting the boy in the car seat and securing the buckle.

"Get in. We'll have to squish together," he told her.

She didn't argue, and he hugged the door frame as much as possible to give her enough room to put on her seat belt.

The moment they were all inside the vehicle, Marc took off. Ryker kept his gaze on the parking lot, as did Duncan.

The black SUV was parked next to the one they'd driven here. Two men dressed in black were disappearing inside the restaurant. He hadn't recognized them, not that he'd expected to. Apparently the Blake-Moore Group had more than enough mercenaries working for them. A never-ending stream of disposable resources, which made him feel sick at heart. Why were these men so anxious to put their lives on the line like this? Didn't they realize how much danger they were placing themselves in? He simply didn't understand it.

"How did they find you?" Marc's question drew him from his dark thoughts.

"I have no idea." He glanced at Olivia who was doing her best to soothe her son. The boy had seemed confused by their abrupt departure, but thankfully wasn't crying.

"What if they've picked up on the fact that we're using the Callahans to back us up?" Duncan turned in his seat to look at Ryker. "First Mike, then Miles and now Marc."

Ryker blew out a breath. "Could be. We all helped Hawk six months ago, including several of the Callahans. It's not a stretch for them to assume we'd use them again."

"I wasn't followed," Marc protested.

"I know you weren't. They showed up minutes before you did." Which was an interesting fact now that he thought about it. "Could they have somehow tapped into your phone?"

Marc let out a snort. "I can't see how they could trace an FBI phone."

"But you use it as your personal device, too." Duncan's tone was mild. "Could be they have your family under surveillance."

"Maybe. I'll call and have one of my colleagues sit on my place, just in case." Clearly Marc didn't want to believe his phone had been traced, but what other explanation was there? Especially considering the mercenaries had beaten him to the restaurant. They had to have had prior knowledge that the place was a meeting point. "But there's been no sign of that. And

I only called the office in Madison to help co-ordinate things."

"Now what?" Olivia's voice held a notice-able tremor.

Ryker reached for her hand. "We'll continue protecting you and Aaron. Just trust us, okay?"

She nodded, and didn't say anything more. But she continued clutching his hand as if it was a lifeline.

"I want to go back to Madison," Marc said. "To the FBI office there."

Olivia tensed, but he nodded his agreement. "Whatever you think is best."

"You know, I'd think they'd have sent more than two men if they knew we'd reached out to the Callahans."

Duncan's observation made him nod. "Yeah, you would think so. Although these guys tend to believe they're better than anyone else."

"Yet we keep proving them wrong," Duncan added thoughtfully. "I wonder if they're run-ning out of men?"

"I sure hope so." That would be the best news ever, in his opinion. What good was the Blake-Moore Group if they only had a handful of men working for them?

Except they wouldn't need any more, would they? Once they had the money Tim and Colin had skimmed from them, the two owners could easily disappear for good.

"Do you think both Harper Moore and Kevin Blake know about the embezzled money? Or just one of them?" Marc asked.

It was a good question. "I don't know. Why? Do you think we can play one owner off the other?" It made sense in a way, to have the entire five million going to one person instead of being split down the middle.

"Maybe." Marc's expression was thoughtful. "Although I can't believe they weren't aware of the gun-selling scheme, which makes me believe they're both in this up to their beady little eyeballs."

"Yeah." And it still burned him to know that while he'd been fighting in Afghanistan, the enemy had used American guns against him and his teammates. "Although, if that's true, why hasn't either one of them been arrested yet?"

Marc met his gaze in the rearview mirror. "From what I hear, there isn't any proof of their culpability. Both Blake and Moore are claiming that their men were acting alone without their knowledge."

"Yeah, right," Duncan muttered.

Marc shrugged. "Once we get the proof we need, they'll both be arrested and charged in federal court. But until then, there isn't much more we can do."

"The money stashed in overseas bank accounts might be the proof we need," Ryker pointed out. "Although we'd have to find a way to trace it back to Colin and Tim. Seth's testimony may help us, there."

"I hope so," Marc agreed.

For several miles no one said anything.

Ryker glanced over at Olivia to see she was resting her head against the edge of Aaron's car seat, her eyes closed. Her fingers still clung to his, so he didn't think she was sleeping.

"Hey, are you okay?" He kept his voice low.

She opened her eyes. "Fine. Except the Braxton-Hicks contractions are back."

He felt the blood drain from his face. "How long have you had them?"

"Since we rushed through the kitchen." She closed her eyes again.

It was the stress of being on the run for their lives. She hadn't said it, but he knew that's what she'd meant. He felt terrible that she was having to go through all of this in her condition.

"Problem?" Marc asked.

He tried not to look as panicked as he felt. "Braxton-Hicks contractions."

"Again?" Duncan swiveled around to face

him, alarm in his gaze. "I don't like this. We need to get her in to see a doctor."

"Couldn't agree more." When Olivia's fingers tightened around his, he looked at her. "What's wrong?"

"Nothing, but I really would like to see a doctor." Her voice was low and steady.

Terror gripped him. "You think this is it? Real labor pains?"

The corner of her mouth tipped up in a half-hearted smile. "No, but I haven't been to see an OB in just over a month, and I'm supposed to go in monthly until I'm four weeks out, then weekly. I've missed one appointment so far, and in another two weeks, it will be two missed appointments."

"That settles it." Ryker wasn't about to take any chances. "Let's find her an OB doctor."

"Where are we?" Olivia frowned as she looked through the window. "I don't recognize this place."

"We're in McFarland, less than fifteen miles outside of Madison," Marc said. "Do you know any OB doctors in Madison?"

"I know Dr. Bowman. He delivered Aaron. I was planning to go to him for this baby, but never had the chance."

"Will he see you without an appointment?"

Ryker cradled her hand between both of his. "Or should we go to the emergency room?"

She wrinkled her nose. "This isn't an emergency. Can you look up his number? Maybe he or one of his associates has an opening."

He reluctantly let her go, then used his phone to pull up the name of the obstetrician. He found the number easily enough and called it, but quickly handed the phone to Olivia as he had no clue what to say.

Olivia politely asked for the next available appointment after explaining that she hadn't been able to see her OB in Illinois as originally planned. After several moments, she said thank you and handed him his phone.

"Tomorrow morning is the earliest they can see me."

"Not today?"

She shrugged. "I'm sure I'll be fine till the morning. They told me to call if anything changes."

A wave of helplessness washed over him. He didn't like it, but what could he do? Other than drive her to the closest hospital and insist she be seen. "That's stupid advice," he mumbled.

"I'll be fine." She rested her head against Aaron's car seat and smoothed her hands over her stomach. "As long as I can relax and remain calm."

He met Marc's concerned gaze in the rearview mirror. Having two kids of his own, Marc was better versed in what a pregnant woman might need.

"We'll find another motel," Marc offered. "We'll stop for a break before I touch base again with the field office here in Madison."

"Yeah, okay." Ryker couldn't seem to tear his gaze from Olivia. Her expression was serene, as if she was deep inside herself, thinking happy thoughts.

If anything happened to her, Aaron or the baby, he'd never forgive himself.

Slow and easy. Breathe in while counting to ten. Breathe out counting to ten.

Olivia repeated the internal monologue over and over, refusing to allow any negative thoughts into her mind. The contractions were already beginning to ease off. She knew God was watching over them and that her baby would be fine.

The SUV stopped and she pried her eyes open, blinking in confusion. After a moment she recognized they were on the outskirts of the city, the state capitol building visible in the distance.

"Just sit tight. We're almost at the hotel," Ryker said.

"Good. I could use a bathroom." Every contraction had only punctuated her need to go. "A suite would be nice if they have one available."

"Not a problem."

The hotels around them seemed nicer than the previous ones they'd stayed in, not that she'd ever complain. All she wanted, needed, was to be safe.

It didn't seem so much to ask.

Think positive, she told herself, drawing in a long, deep breath. They were safe. She had three men watching over them, one of them a federal agent no less. Between God and Ryker, she couldn't be in better hands.

"How about that one?" Marc gestured to a hotel a few miles ahead.

"Fine with me," Ryker agreed.

"Anything that nice will require a driver's license and credit card on file," Duncan pointed out.

"I know."

A twinge of concern had her meeting Ryker's gaze. "Do you think that's wise?"

"Don't worry—we'll keep you safe." Ryker's smile was reassuring and she didn't doubt his sincerity. He'd done nothing but keep her and Aaron safe since the moment they'd met.

Three days ago? It seemed much longer.

She felt bad that protecting her had become

such a monstrous job. Logically, she knew it wasn't her fault Colin had put the stupid account information in her diaper bag. And her brother and Tim had skimmed the money from their employer in the first place.

Five million. She still couldn't quite comprehend that much money.

A contraction tightened her belly and she drew in a slow, deep breath. No stress, remember? She repeated her mantra as Marc navigated the busy Madison traffic.

When Marc passed the hotel, a niggle of fear encroached her inner peace. "What's wrong?"

"Just taking precautions," Marc responded.

She frowned when she noticed the silent look Marc and Ryker exchanged. Being wedged as she was between Ryker and Aaron's car seat, she couldn't see behind them.

"Are we being followed?"

"Please try not to worry." Ryker rested his hand on her knee. "We're just being careful."

No, there was more to it. The tension between the men had risen sharply over the past five minutes.

Breathe in—count to ten. Breathe out—count to ten.

It wasn't working. Marc took a quick left turn, then a right. The jerky movements weren't helping her discomfort.

"Head out of town," Ryker said. "It'll be easier to pick up a tail with fewer cars on the road."

"I'm trying." Marc seemed to be concentrating on the road before him.

"I wanna get out," Aaron cried, picking up on the tension between the adults. "I hav'ta go to the bathroom."

She did too, but had been doing her best to ignore the urge. "Soon, Aaron."

Aaron kicked his feet and she suppressed a sigh. Remaining calm and peaceful under these circumstances was impossible.

The cars thinned out around them, and just as she was about to breathe a sigh of relief, Marc pressed the accelerator, picking up speed.

"What is it?"

"Black SUV with tinted windows, but could be nothing," Duncan said. "We're just trying to put distance between us and them."

Oh no, not again. Please, not again!

Marc increased their speed another notch, making her wonder if the black SUV was keeping pace. She wanted to turn in her seat to look out the window, but couldn't.

Another contraction tightened across her belly and she caught her breath at the intensity of it. It was stronger than the Braxton-Hicks she'd been experiencing until now.

Please, God, keep my baby safe!

She breathed through the contraction, trying to imagine the sound of ocean waves hitting the sandy shore. She had one of those white-noise machines and the wave sound was her favorite.

"They're closing the gap. We need to call for backup." Marc picked up his phone from the center console and handed it to Duncan. "Call 911 first, then I'll get in touch with the FBI field office."

While Duncan spoke into the phone in a low, urgent tone, she reached for Ryker's hand. "Pray with me." She looked up at him. "Please?"

"Of course." He cleared his throat. "Dear Lord, keep all of us safe in Your care."

"Guide us on Your chosen path," she added, "and show us the way to escape these men. Amen."

"Amen," Ryker echoed.

For several long moments there was nothing but silence, then suddenly Marc shouted, "Brace yourselves!"

Before she had a chance to react, something hard hit the back of their SUV, jarring them. Marc fought to keep control of the wheel, even as he picked up speed. He moved from one lane to the other, in an attempt to avoid the vehicle behind them.

Another contraction tightened her stomach and she felt a stab of fear.

What if this wasn't false labor? What if she was about to have her baby five and a half weeks early? She told herself that less than six weeks wasn't the end of the world, but that was under normal circumstances.

And these were anything but.

FOURTEEN

The crunch of metal hitting metal was jarring. The vehicle rocked a bit, but Marc kept it under control. Ryker clenched his jaw, hating how vulnerable they were. It was disturbing to know Olivia and Aaron were in danger. The police needed to get here, and soon!

"Mommy, I'm scared." Aaron began to cry.

"Shh, we're okay." Olivia's tone lacked conviction as she reassured her son.

Marc hit the accelerator, hard, doing his best to get them away from the SUV behind them.

"Is there a place we can go to get away? An off-ramp, maybe?" Ryker knew it wasn't likely. The highway up ahead only showed woods flanking the road.

They'd left the city limits far behind.

"I'm trying." Marc continued pushing the speed even faster, which was also worrisome if they were to be hit from behind again. If Marc lost control of the vehicle, they could all die.

"The police are on the way," Duncan said.

"They better be." Ryker couldn't help turning to look back at the SUV. Marc had gotten some distance away, but their attackers were doing their best to close the gap. "Step on it, Marc."

"I am." Marc sounded tense, too.

Olivia moaned softly under her breath and he felt a stab of fear. "What's wrong?"

"Nothing." She bit the word out between clenched teeth and the way she held on to her stomach was concerning.

"More Braxton-Hicks contractions?" He didn't want to believe she was truly in labor. It wasn't time for the baby to be born yet.

"I don't think so." Her voice was strained. "These might be real."

"Real?" Duncan twisted in his seat to face them. "No way."

Olivia didn't answer, clearly concentrating on what she was experiencing. The fact that she didn't continue to talk to Aaron said volumes.

"You need to get us out of danger, Marc." Ryker hated feeling helpless, and sitting next to Olivia without being the one behind the wheel was driving him nuts.

"I'm trying," Marc repeated as he shifted their car into the left lane to go around a pickup truck. The driver shot them a dirty look, which

Marc ignored. The SUV followed them into the left lane, keeping pace.

Ryker swallowed hard and silently repeated the prayer he and Olivia had shared moments ago.

Dear Lord, keep all of us safe in Your care... show us the way to escape these men. Amen.

A minute later, the wail of sirens filled the air. Ryker craned his neck, trying to locate the source of the sound. Highways were under the control of the Wisconsin State Patrol and he hoped they'd arrive soon.

"There!" Duncan must have been on the lookout for them, too. He gestured to the side-view mirror. "They're about three miles back, but coming up from behind."

"The police will save us, right?" Aaron asked.

"For sure." Ryker smiled at the little boy, then peered back over his shoulder. He still couldn't see the police from this angle. But he did notice the black SUV abruptly slow down and veer into the right lane. "Hey, I think Blake-Moore is giving up the chase."

"I hope so." Marc's voice was calmer now. "Can you make out the license plate?"

Ryker narrowed his gaze, trying to see the letters and numbers. It wasn't easy since they were going so fast and the SUV was slowing down. "Frank, Oscar, Tom…" He sighed. "I can't see the rest. They're exiting the highway."

"Call dispatch. Let them know what we have on the license plate so far," Marc said.

Duncan spoke into the phone again as Marc gently slowed his speed. Within seconds, the police car came up behind them.

Marc pulled over to the shoulder and stopped the car. He peeled his fingers from the steering wheel, but kept his hands visible after pulling out his badge and lowering the driver's-side window.

"FBI Special Agent Marc Callahan," he said as the state patrol officer approached. He opened his badge so the trooper could look at it more closely.

"And I'm with the Milwaukee PD, Officer Duncan O'Hare," Duncan added. "I made the 911 call."

"I saw the dent in your rear bumper and just heard the first three letters of the license plate number come through over the radio." The state patrol officer bent forward to look into the back seat of the vehicle. "Who are you?"

"Former army Sergeant Ryker Tillman," he introduced himself, using his military background, rather than his security-consulting business. "And this is Olivia and Aaron." He purposefully left off their last names.

"Hi, Mr. Police man." Aaron's initial fright after being hit by the SUV seemed to have faded under the novelty of having the police arrive.

"Hi." The patrol officer flashed a quick smile.

"As you can see, Olivia is pregnant and having contractions," Ryker continued. "We need to get her to the closest hospital as soon as possible."

"Contractions?" The patrol officer appeared taken aback by the news. "Hey, no one mentioned a pregnant woman and a kid."

"My fault," Duncan said, although Ryker knew he'd omitted the details about Olivia and Aaron on purpose. "I was just so worried we'd crash. Thanks for getting here so quickly."

The patrolman looked at Marc who had replaced his badge in his pocket. "Are you working a case? Is that why you were targeted?"

"I am on a case, yes, and this incident may be related." Marc shrugged. "I have a call in to the FBI office in Madison. I'd like to discuss this with them first, before I give you additional details."

The patrol officer frowned. "The attempt to run you off the road happened in my jurisdiction."

"I know, and I very much appreciate your quick response." Marc's smile was strained. "I'm happy to give you more information as soon as I run it through official channels. You know how the upper brass is. They always have to be in charge. They act like those of us with boots on the ground can't make a decision, which is bull."

"True that." The patrol officer must have appreciated Marc's honesty, as he nodded and handed over a business card. "Okay, Agent Callahan. I'll expect to hear from you soon. In the meantime, we have a BOLO out on the black SUV with a partial plate of Frank, Oscar, Tom." The guy hesitated, then added, "You want a police escort to the hospital?"

"I think we're okay, but if you'd put the word out to the other patrol officers, I'd appreciate it."

"Will do." He tipped his hat.

"Thanks again." Marc rolled up his window and waited for the trooper to return to his squad car before easing their SUV back onto the interstate.

"Where to? Do we need to go to the Madison FBI office?" Ryker could tell Olivia was still experiencing contractions.

"No, the hospital." Marc met his gaze in the rearview mirror. "I want Olivia to be seen by a doctor ASAP."

"Me, too." He took Olivia's hand in his. "You'll go to the ER, won't you?"

"Yes." The way she readily went along with

the plan only emphasized the seriousness of the situation. Olivia would never agree to be seen unless she was truly concerned about her condition.

About the baby's condition.

Ryker listened to her deep, rhythmic breathing, hoping, praying that this was nothing more than Braxton-Hicks brought on by stress. Being rear-ended by the Blake-Moore SUV could have made the contractions worse, right?

Maybe now that they were safe, at least for the moment, the contractions would stop.

Olivia's hand tightened over his, killing his feeble hope. The tightness corresponded with whatever new contraction she was experiencing. Her grip remained tight around his hand until the pain eased.

Oh yeah, there was no doubt about it.

Olivia was in labor.

He closed his eyes on a wave of despair, knowing he'd almost failed in his mission to keep her, Aaron and the baby safe.

The contractions were a good ten minutes apart, but strong enough to steal her breath.

"Where's the closest hospital?" Ryker asked.

"Not any hospital," she protested. She shifted in her seat, trying to get into a more comfortable position. "I want to go to the teaching hospital where my original OB works."

She sensed Ryker's impatience. "It's too far away."

"I have time—the contractions aren't that close. Besides, if this baby is coming early I want to be in the best hospital with the best neonatal intensive care unit." She gritted her teeth as her abdomen tightened with another contraction. "Go back to Madison."

"The baby?" Aaron's innocent question drew her attention.

"Yes, sweetie. Soon you're going to have a baby brother or baby sister."

"I wanna baby brother," Aaron announced.

She didn't have the heart to tell him she suspected the baby was a girl. She tried to smile. "You're going to be Mommy's helper with the baby, aren't you?"

"Yep." Aaron nodded.

The pain intensified and she found herself grabbing Ryker's hand again as she breathed through it. It was always easier to practice in those birthing classes than to actually do it. She remembered getting upset with Tim when she was in labor with Aaron, because he kept telling her she was breathing wrong. She'd finally yelled at him not to tell her how to breathe. Instead of apologizing, Tim had plopped into a chair and sulked.

Unlike Ryker, who tried to be supportive. He didn't say anything, his gaze stricken with guilt and fear as if he had never planned to be around long enough to see her give birth.

Yeah, big surprise.

But he let her squeeze his hand without making a sound of protest, brushing a kiss across her knuckles when the pain eased.

"You're doing great," he said encouragingly.

"I'm not sure I have much of a choice." Her attempt at humor was weak. "Baby has a mind of her own."

"Just like her mommy," Ryker agreed.

That made her smile. She was touched by his willingness to support her through this.

"We're fifteen minutes from Madison." Marc caught her gaze. "Sure you're okay?"

"Positive." Although she was worried about Aaron. "Ryker, will you watch Aaron for me?"

"Hey, why don't I give Mike and Shayla a call," Duncan offered. "If Brodie is feeling better, maybe they'll watch Aaron. Brodie is just a little older than Aaron. I'm sure they'll have fun playing together."

"Can I play with Brodie?" Aaron asked.

"If he's feeling better, sure." She glanced at

Ryker. "You may need to stay close to Aaron. He trusts you."

Ryker hesitated, then nodded. "If Mike can't help, I will. But I'd like to be there for you, Olivia."

It was the sweetest thing he'd ever said to her and it made her eyes mist with tears. "Watching Aaron will help me."

"Okay." He lightly rubbed his thumb over the back of her hand. "Whatever you want."

The stark contrast between Ryker and Tim was obvious. Was Ryker always like this? Or was this an exception under dramatically stressful and dangerous circumstances? She didn't know for sure, but would be forever grateful for his steadfast support.

"Hey, Mike, it's Dunc. How's Brodie? Better? That's great." She listened as Duncan made arrangements for Mike, Shayla and Brodie to meet them in Madison and take care of Olivia's son.

"Let me know when you're close," Duncan said. "I'll give you the details when we know them."

"All set?" Ryker asked when Duncan disconnected from the call.

"Yep. Brodie must have had a twenty-four-hour bug, because he's fine now." Duncan flashed a grin at Aaron. "He's looking forward to meeting you."

Olivia began to relax. Trust Ryker, Duncan and the Callahans to come to the rescue.

She breathed through another contraction, just as they arrived in the ER. Ryker helped her out of the back seat, and it was difficult to leave Aaron behind with Marc and Duncan, even though she knew the two men would keep him safe.

"You're in labor?" The triage nurse wasted no time. "Let's get you back to a room right away."

Ryker came with her, and the nurse assumed he was the father of the baby. "Dad, have a seat here, while the doctor examines your wife."

Olivia opened her mouth to correct them, but Ryker quickly shook his head. "Don't worry, sweetheart, I'll be right next to you the entire time."

"Okay." She understood he wanted her to play along, and why not? Honestly, she needed Ryker's support now more than ever.

The doctor asked a series of questions then performed a quick exam. "No sign of the baby's head yet, so that's good. We have an OB on her way down. She'll be here in a minute. We're also getting you a bed up in Labor and Delivery."

"So, she's really going to have the baby today?" Ryker's tone rose in surprise.

"It's possible, but Dr. Regner will know more. Oh, there she is now."

Dr. Regner flashed a reassuring smile as she entered the room, then proceeded to ask her the same questions she'd just answered for the ER doctor. The only difference was that Dr. Regner's exam was more thorough. "Okay, you're about three centimeters dilated. Once we get you settled in Labor and Delivery, we'll put a monitor on the baby so we can see how he or she is doing."

"But aren't you going to do something to stop the contractions?" Olivia had assumed they'd want her bun to stay in the oven a little longer.

"You're early but I'd estimate the baby is roughly five pounds. We'll do an ultrasound to be sure."

The next hour passed in a flurry of activity. When she arrived in the labor and delivery room, the nurse started an IV to provide fluids. Once that happened, her contractions slowed way down.

"I might not be in labor after all." She glanced at Ryker who'd remained at her side through the IV and the ultrasound. "The contractions seem to have stopped."

"That happens sometimes once you're rehydrated," the nurse said. "But if it's true labor, they'll return."

Olivia secretly hoped they wouldn't return, at least not for another couple of weeks.

When the nurse finally left them alone, Ryker leaned over and took her hand. "I want you to know Marc has an FBI agent by the name of Tony Seavers from the Madison office stationed outside your door for protection."

"Really? I'm sure that's not necessary."

"Yes, it is. And I've heard from Mike that Brodie and Aaron are getting along great. Since you were admitted, Mike and Shayla took Aaron home with them."

"That's good to know." She could rest easier, knowing her son was in good hands. "Although all of this fuss may be for nothing, since the contractions seem to have stopped."

"Wait and see what Dr. Regner says, okay?" Ryker bowed his head for a moment, before meeting her gaze. "I'm just glad we made it here safely. I was worried you might deliver this baby in the car."

"Nah, she's too stubborn for that." Olivia tried to make light of the situation, but truthfully, she'd had the same fear. "Thanks for staying with me."

"Of course." His gaze turned serious. "I'd never let you go through this all alone, Olivia."

Tears pricked her eyes again. Hormones. And maybe something more. She cared about Ryker, way too much. Her head knew he was just being nice, her knight in shining armor, rescuing her from certain danger, but her heart yearned for something more.

His love.

A contraction tightened her belly, making her suck in a harsh breath. "I guess I was wrong."

"About?"

"They're back. The contractions, I mean." She concentrated on breathing.

"Easy now," Ryker crooned. "Do you want me to get the nurse?"

"In a minute." She rode the crest of the contraction, then relaxed as the pain eased.

Ryker's phone rang. He gave her hand a quick pat, then stood. "I'll answer this and get the nurse, okay?"

"Okay." She wasn't going to argue. If the baby insisted on coming early, then she needed to be prepared.

Ryker left the room. She imagined him chatting briefly with the FBI agent outside her door before moving on.

When her door opened, she turned her head to greet the nurse. Only it wasn't the nurse standing there. It was Tim's cousin Seth Willis.

Her blood ran cold for a moment, as she registered the fact that Seth was wearing a uniform and a name tag identifying him as a hospital security guard. "What do you want?"

Seth didn't answer, but the flatness in his eyes reminded her of Tim. She reached for her call button a second too late. Seth slammed one hand over her mouth, the other pinning her wrists together in a painful grip.

Kicking the side rail with her foot, she tried to make as much noise as possible. But to no avail.

With Seth's hand over her mouth, it was impossible to breathe. The room spun. No! This couldn't be happening. Where was the FBI? Ryker? The nurse?

Please, Lord, help me! Save me and my baby!

FIFTEEN

Ryker paced the hallway as Marc updated him on the SUV that had tried to run them off the interstate. "We found it abandoned at the side of the road, wiped clean. Not a single fingerprint or piece of trace evidence."

"Figures." They really needed a break, some way to get directly to Kevin Blake and Harper Moore. They were the ones behind these attempts against Olivia and he wanted them held responsible. "Anything else?"

"We're working with local law enforcement to find Blake and Moore but so far we don't have any idea where they are. The good news is that the banking information is legit. Our team was able to track down the embezzled funds with an electronic trail back to the Blake-Moore Group. Once we get our hands on Blake and Moore, we should have what we need to arrest them."

"Good." Ryker heard a muffled thump and

urned toward the door of Olivia's room. Tony
Seavers, the FBI agent posted there on guard
duty, abruptly turned and pushed open her door
and let out a shout.

"Hey! Get away from her!"

Shoving the phone in his pocket without dis-
connecting from the call, Ryker ran into Oliv-
a's room hot on Tony's heels. When he realized
Tony was pulling a man off Olivia, he ran toward them. His blood ran hot when he saw it
was Seth Willis.

He grabbed on to Seth, helping to pull him
away. Between them, he and Tony wrestled Wil-
is to the floor and cuffed him.

"What are you doing, Seth? I thought you
wanted to turn your life around." Ryker didn't
hide the anger in his tone. "What did you hope
o accomplish by hurting Olivia?"

"I didn't want to hurt her. I just wanted the
bank-account information." Seth glared at him.
"If she had handed it over, I would have left her
alone."

Ryker couldn't believe he'd bought into the
guy's story about going straight. That he'd ac-
ually given Willis the phone information for
Dennis Ludwig, their FBI contact.

"Ryker!" Hearing his name from his pocket,
he realized Marc Callahan was still on the
phone.

"Seth Willis tried to attack Olivia," he said into the phone. "I'll call you back." Without waiting for a response, he ended the call and rushed over to Olivia, raking his gaze over her. Her cheeks were pink, her hair disheveled and her breathing seemed labored. "Are you hurt?"

"I'm not sure. Please get the nurse." Both of her hands were splayed over her belly. "I'm not having any contractions and I'm worried something is wrong."

No way was he leaving. He reached over and pushed the call button. "The nurse is on her way. Please, Olivia, I need to know if he hurt you."

She shook her head. "Scared me more than anything, because I couldn't breathe. I kept kicking the side rails, hoping to make enough noise to attract attention. I knocked him off-balance, which helped."

His jaw tightened when he saw her bare feet, imagining the bruises that would likely mar her beautiful skin within the next day or so.

"I heard you." Tony Seavers finished zip-tying Seth's ankles then came over to stand beside Ryker. "I'm so sorry. When he claimed to be Olivia's husband's cousin, I didn't think to question him. Especially since he works here in security. Why wouldn't he be legit?"

Ryker wanted to snap at the Fed, but reined in his temper. This was his fault for not checking to see if this was the hospital where Seth worked. Not to mention believing the guy's innocence in the first place. "It's okay." He shot a glare at Seth who was propped in the corner of the room. "But I want him booked for assault and battery."

"Agreed. I'll call in the local law enforcement now. They can take him into custody." Tony's gaze lingered on Olivia for a moment, obviously still feeling guilty for his role in her attack, before stepping away to use his phone.

Olivia's smile was wan. "Don't blame Tony. Seth didn't lie. He is my dead husband's cousin."

"I know." Ryker lowered his chin to his chest, trying to get a grip. Normally he abhorred violence, but at this moment he wanted to punch Seth in the jaw for daring to place his hands on Olivia. For putting both an innocent woman and her unborn child in danger. He lifted his head. "I don't blame Tony. This is my fault, Olivia. I hope you can forgive me."

"Your fault? Funny, it seems to me Seth was the one who attacked me."

It was nice of her to try letting him off the hook, but he knew the truth. He turned toward Seth. "The Feds have the banking information, so hurting Olivia wasn't necessary."

Seth looked away, unable to hold his gaze.

There was a slight knock at the door, before it

opened revealing a woman in scrubs. "I'm your nurse, Olivia. What can I do for you?"

Ryker reluctantly moved away from Olivia's bedside to make room for the nurse. He crossed over to Willis. "Tell me the truth. Are you still working for Blake-Moore?"

Seth hunched his shoulders. "No. I told you, I didn't want to put my life on the line for them. You were right that they treat us as disposable assets, easily replaced."

"You came here to assault an innocent woman, all on your own? Blake-Moore didn't put you up to this?" He was hoping Willis might be able to contact one of the owners to set up a sting, but it didn't seem likely.

"Yeah, I came on my own. Five million is a lot of cash." Willis thrust out his jaw toward Olivia. "Why should she get it all?"

"I told you the Feds have the banking information." He repeated the words slowly, hoping they would sink into Seth's tiny brain. "The money is evidence of a crime, not to mention motive for hurting Olivia. No one is going to be spending that money, do you understand?"

Seth's expression turned uncertain. "So this was all for nothing?"

"Exactly. Your greed will land you in jail, you moron." Ryker turned his back on the guy, unable to stand looking at him. Instead, he listened to what the nurse was saying.

"—doctor. She'll decide the next steps."

He edged closer. "What's going on?"

"Looks like you'll have to wait awhile to become a daddy," the nurse told him. "She doesn't seem to be having any more contractions."

"But the baby is okay?"

"So far, so good. I'll talk to the doctor. She may want to keep your wife here longer or send her home. We'll see what Dr. Regner thinks."

The nurse left as the local police arrived to take Seth into custody. They wanted a statement from Olivia, who provided her story.

"Listen, I'll fill you in on the rest," Ryker said, when they pressed her for more information on the bank accounts. "She doesn't need additional stress right now. All you need to know right now is that Seth Willis attacked her."

"We need to understand the motive behind this," the officer argued.

"Here, call Marc Callahan. He's with the FBI. He can provide more details."

The officer reluctantly took Marc's cell number, then cut the zip ties around Seth's ankles and hauled him to his feet.

When Ryker was alone with Olivia, he bent down and kissed her forehead.

"I'm sorry," he repeated. "I hope the stress of all of this isn't going to hurt you or the baby."

"I was having contractions before Seth came in here." She grimaced and put a hand on her belly. "I can't deny feeling worried about how the baby is doing. Hopefully the added stress doesn't cause any harm."

Her words hit hard. She was right; the stress she'd suffered not just today but throughout the past few days hadn't helped one bit.

Ryker almost sank to his knees in despair. If her baby suffered any untoward complications from being born too early, he'd never forgive himself.

The contractions had completely disappeared, and for some reason, that bothered her more than the idea of having the baby arrive early. Olivia was doing her best not to show her panic and fear, but it wasn't easy.

None of this was Ryker's fault, but he looked so upset and miserable, she knew he was still blaming himself.

"Will you stay with me?" She reached for his hand. "Whatever the doctor decides to do, I can't bear the thought of delivering this baby alone."

"Yes." His simple statement warmed her heart. "I won't leave you."

"Thanks." Over his shoulder, she was relieved to see Dr. Regner enter the room.

"I hear your contractions have stopped." Dr. Regner's voice was cheerful. "I've been watching your baby's heartbeat on the monitor, and everything is looking great. I'd like to continue observing you for a bit longer, just to be sure you don't unexpectedly go back into labor."

"I don't feel great." Olivia tried not to show her fear. "Are you sure the baby will be okay?"

"Your ultrasound confirms the baby's at five pounds. That's plenty far enough along to avoid serious complications. Besides, babies under stress often develop their lungs faster." Dr. Regner patted her arm. "If the baby decides to come early, you'll both be just fine. I'd like to do a quick exam, okay?"

"Sure."

Ryker stepped back to provide her some privacy, and she reluctantly let go of his hand. The exam was over in moments.

"You're still dilated at three centimeters." Dr. Regner pursed her lips thoughtfully. "No progress there, so it seems like your baby has decided to stay put for a little while longer."

"Really?" Ryker's expression brightened with hope. "So no premature baby?"

"Not yet." Dr. Regner's tone held a note of caution. "But I'd like to keep Olivia here, maybe until dinnertime. If the contractions don't start up by then, we'll consider discharging her."

Olivia should have been relieved at the news, but she had to swallow a protest. Of course she didn't want her baby to be born prematurely, but on the other hand, she was hesitant to be back outside the walls of the hospital where Blake-Moore would have yet another chance to come after her.

"What's wrong?" Ryker's voice was soft. "You look upset."

"I'm not. It's just... I feel safer here at the hospital with you and the FBI agent standing outside my door. I'm not sure I want to leave."

His brow furrowed. "I'm surprised to hear you say that, especially after the way Seth managed to get in here."

"But he was a hospital employee and I think Tony will be hypervigilant from this point forward." The poor guy was beating himself up as much as Ryker was, both of them shouldering the guilt over Seth's attack.

Seth was the bad guy here. A man callous enough to roughly hold down a pregnant woman.

Ryker stared at her for a long moment. "Do you want me to ask the doctor to keep you here overnight?"

"No, she won't do that, not if it's not medically necessary to keep me. Besides, I can't take up a bed some other woman in labor might need." Olivia forced a smile. "I'm being overly emotional about this. I'll be fine."

"You're being honest," Ryker countered. "And I can't blame you for feeling safer here than in a motel with me. I've done a poor job of protecting you."

"No! That's not what I meant at all." She tugged on his hand. "Stop putting words in my mouth. Aaron and I are alive right now because you put your life on the line for us, more than once." Her eyes misted. "I owe you a deep debt of gratitude."

"Don't." His voice was low and gravelly. He reached up to wipe away a stray tear with his thumb. "I can't stand seeing you cry."

That made her chuckle. "Guess you haven't spent much time around pregnant women, huh?"

"No, I haven't." There was a brief pause before he added, "I dated a single mom, but she and her young daughter were killed while I was in Afghanistan."

She sucked in a harsh breath. "Killed? How? Why?"

"Carjacking gone bad." His tone held a note of bitterness. "We had only been seeing each other a few months, but her death hit me hard, haunting me for a long time. Mostly because if

I had been here with her, she and her daughter would be alive today."

"Oh, Ryker." She suddenly understood him a little better. Losing his girlfriend and her child must have been the impetus for him to come searching for her and Aaron. He'd assigned himself as her personal guardian angel. "You don't know that for certain."

"Yes, I do."

She sadly shook her head. "Ryker, you could have been anywhere other than Afghanistan. Try to place your trust in God's plan for us. I'm sorry your girlfriend and her daughter died, but you must know they're in a better place now. You need to have faith."

"It doesn't seem fair that Cheri and Cyndi had to die so young. Why would God do something like that?" His expression betrayed his frustration and angst.

"I know it's not always easy to understand God's plan. All we can do is pray for strength and guidance. We need to place our worries in His hands."

"Maybe." His tone held a note of doubt.

She squeezed his hand. "I am."

Ryker's gaze turned curious. "Is that what you've been doing while you've been here in the hospital?"

She was surprised by his question. "Of

course. I've been praying nonstop since the moment Willa brought me into her church, welcoming me and Aaron with open arms. Praying brings me a sense of peace, as if God is assuring me that He's watching over us."

"I've never in my life prayed with anyone, until you." Ryker's soft admission tugged at her heart. "I hope God continues to grant me the ability to keep you and your baby safe."

"He will." She didn't doubt it for a moment. "And I'm happy to hear you saying that. It means a lot to me that you're discovering the power of prayer."

Her heart swelled with hope and love. Liv cared about Ryker so much, but reminded herself not to overreact. Having just learned about Ryker's past, she understood that she and Aaron were nothing more than a poor substitute for Cheri and Cyndi, the woman and little girl he'd once loved.

Still, she was blessed to have Ryker with her now. To have him staying at her side through the birth of her baby. Although, it was looking more and more like she wouldn't be having this baby today.

A knock at her door brought her out of her reverie. "Come in."

Ryker turned, putting himself between the

doorway and her bed, but his protection wasn't needed. Her nurse popped into the room.

"Time for me to take your vitals." As the nurse busied herself with the blood-pressure cuff, she glanced down at Olivia. "I hear Dr. Regner is planning to discharge you in a few hours."

"Yes. Apparently my baby is being stubborn and wants to stay inside a bit longer." She rubbed her hand over her belly, avoiding the monitor strapped there picking up the baby's heartbeat.

"Well, that happens sometimes." The nurse listened to her blood pressure, took her pulse then stuck an electric thermometer under her tongue. "Dr. Regner is preparing the discharge paperwork now, so if all goes well, you'll be out of here in time for dinner." The nurse winked. "Maybe you can get your husband to take you out someplace fancy."

Since her admission, the staff had assumed she and Ryker were husband and wife, and neither one of them had said or done anything to correct them. It seemed a bit dishonest, but Olivia didn't want Ryker to leave, so she played along, forcing a smile. When the nurse removed the thermometer probe, she said, "Maybe I will."

"Absolutely. I'll take you anywhere you'd like to go," Ryker agreed, lifting her hand to kiss her knuckles. A shiver rippled up her arm and she hoped he didn't notice her innate response to his touch.

"Aw, you two are so sweet together." The nurse beamed, before turning and then leaving the room. "Call if you need anything," she added over her shoulder.

The minute the door closed, she glanced up at Ryker. "I can't help feeling guilty about not telling them the truth."

"I know, but what's the harm? Whether we're married or not, I'm here to support you. And there's no way in the world I'm leaving you alone."

"I guess." She knew he was right, but secretly wondered if every reference to them as a couple made him feel a bit panicky.

After all, this wasn't exactly what he'd bargained for when he'd come to find her. Yet he hadn't turned away.

Just the opposite.

He'd held her, kissed her and cared for her.

The fact that she wanted more, wanted it all, was her problem. Not his.

She needed to remember that once Kevin Blake and Harper Moore were in custody, she and Ryker would go their separate ways.

SIXTEEN

Ryker didn't mind others assuming he was Olivia's husband and the father of her baby. In fact, he rather liked it. Sure, he knew this was just a temporary situation for them. Once Olivia was safe, she wouldn't need him anymore.

But for now, he intended to be there for her. To support her through this. No woman should have to go through childbirth alone.

Maybe once the danger was over, she'd continue to allow him to stop by and visit, to help her with Aaron. Having a new baby and a three-year-old would be stressful. Even if she was able to sell the house and use the money to live on for a while, she'd need emotional support.

It was humbling to realize she felt safer here in the hospital, despite the way Seth had gotten to her. Maybe part of her feeling safe had to do with having access to immediate medical care. He made a mental note to ask Dr. Regner if she wouldn't consider keeping Olivia at least overnight. If the answer was no, then fine. He'd work out some sort of plan with Marc Callahan and the Feds. Now that the FBI was involved, they should be able to keep a cocoon of security around Olivia and Aaron.

"Ryker? Do you think I could talk to Aaron?" Her tone was wistful. "I haven't been away from him for this length of time since we escaped from the motel room last Christmas."

With a nod, he pulled out his phone. "Sure, here's Mike's number."

She gratefully took the phone and asked Mike to use the app that allowed Aaron to see her face. "Hey, Aaron, how are you doing?"

"Hi, Mommy." Aaron waved and leaned toward the screen as if to see her better. "Where are you?"

"I'm at the hospital, but your little brother or sister isn't going to be born today after all. Guess you'll have to wait a bit longer to meet him or her."

"I wanna baby brother." Aaron's steadfast belief in his ability to impact the gender of her baby made Ryker smile. If Olivia was right about having a girl, he hoped the little boy wouldn't be too disappointed.

"I know you do, but God is the one who decides if I'm having a boy or a girl, remember?"

Olivia smiled at her son. "And you're going to be an awesome big brother no matter what."

Aaron nodded. "Yep. Brodie and I are playing dinosaurs." He picked up a plastic T. rex, showing her.

"I'm glad you're having fun. Be good for Brodie's mommy and daddy, okay?"

"I am good." Aaron's eyes widened with innocence. "You can ask them."

"I will ask them," Olivia agreed firmly.

"When are you coming to get me?" Aaron's voice was plaintive.

"Soon, baby. When the doctor says I can go home, we'll come pick you up."

"Or Mr. and Mrs. Callahan will come meet us," Ryker added. "We'll let you know, okay?"

"Okay." For a moment Aaron looked as if he might cry, but then Shayla's voice could be heard in the background. "Who wants to help make chocolate-chip cookies?"

"Me!" Aaron and Brodie both shouted at the same time. "Bye, Mommy." The little boy ran out of view of the screen, replaced by Mike.

"He's fine, Olivia." Mike's gaze was reassuring. "We're keeping a close eye on him."

"I know you are. Thank you so much." Olivia looked as if she might cry again. "We'll let you know when the doctor discharges me."

Mike hesitated, then nodded. "Sure thing. Although it might be better for Aaron to stay with us for a while longer."

Ryker secretly agreed but Olivia looked distressed. "Oh, I don't know about that," she was quick to say. "He hasn't been away from me overnight before."

"How about we talk about it later?" Ryker gave Mike a slight nod. "First we need to find a safe house of some sort. Hopefully the FBI has something we can use."

"Absolutely. Just give us a call. Later." Mike disconnected from the call.

Olivia reluctantly passed Ryker his phone. "I'm glad Aaron seems to be doing okay."

"I'm sure he's having fun playing with Brodie." He took her hand again. "How are you feeling? Any contractions?"

"Not since just before Seth came in." She looked from their joined hands to meet his gaze. "You really think the FBI will provide a safe house for me?"

"Yes. You're a key witness, Olivia. Your testimony of finding the bank-account information, and the fact that men employed by Blake-Moore came after you in order to get it, will assist in putting Blake and Moore behind bars."

"I guess." She didn't look convinced. "But we haven't really proven that the men who came after us worked for Blake-Moore. I'm worried they'll get off on some sort of technicality."

"They won't." He was going to do everything in his power to make sure that didn't happen. "Try not to worry about that, okay? Just stay focused on your baby."

"I will." There was a steely determination in her tone.

His phone rang, and he recognized Marc Callahan's number. "It's Marc." He released her hand and turned from her bedside. "Hey, what's going on?"

"We just started questioning the mercenary you captured at the motel. He gave us his name, James Corrian, but other than that, he's not talking. Apparently he's not willing to give up his bosses. A lawyer just showed up, likely paid for by the Blake-Moore Group."

He blew out a frustrated breath. "Corrian has to know that he'll do a significant amount of jail time. Did you offer to cut him a deal if he talked?"

"Yes, but he wasn't interested. His trust in Blake-Moore is misplaced. Could be he'll need to spend time behind bars before he realizes it's better to provide evidence against them and save himself."

"Unfortunately, we don't have that kind of time." Ryker didn't like where this was going.

"We need those guys behind bars now, not in three months."

"We'll keep trying," Marc assured him. "Ludwig is flying in from DC to help provide resources to find Blake and Moore. Don't forget, we have Willis, too. Maybe we'll get more from him."

"I hope so." But Ryker wasn't really convinced of that. Seth Willis had come here to get the bank information for his own selfish reasons. It wasn't as if Blake-Moore had sent him. The fact that he'd worked full-time as a hospital security guard was evidence that Willis had left the Blake-Moore Group. "When will you question Seth?"

"Heading that way now."

Ryker glanced at Olivia who was clearly listening to his side of the conversation. As much as he wanted to shield her from what was going on, she deserved to know. "Good, keep me posted. Also, it looks like Olivia may be discharged from the hospital in a couple of hours. We're going to need a safe place to go. Have anything in mind?"

"Good question. I'll see what we can come up with. Even if we just end up going to a motel, we'll have an FBI agent assigned to her protection detail."

Just one? Ryker would have felt better with at

least three additional men. Granted, he'd have Duncan's help, too, so maybe they'd be okay. "I'll let you know when she's discharged."

Ryker disconnected and tucked the phone back into his pocket.

"We're never going to get anyone to turn on Blake-Moore." Olivia looked forlorn.

"We will. Just remember at the end of the day, everyone has their own survival instinct. Someone will turn on them." He crossed over, pulled up a chair and sat down beside her. "You're the one who told me to have faith in God's plan, remember?"

A smile tugged at the corner of her mouth. "Yes, I remember. I guess sometimes it's easier to give advice than to take it."

"Exactly." She was so beautiful, he longed to kiss her. To hold her close, reassure her that everything was going to be all right. Anyone trying to hurt her would have to go through him.

He didn't mind putting his life on the line to protect her.

The nurse returned for another set of vital signs. A few minutes later, the doctor came in. Ryker went to the far corner of the room to give Olivia privacy.

"Still at three centimeters," Dr. Regner announced. "I'm going to go ahead and discharge you. There's no point in waiting. You're not in active labor."

Ryker squelched a flash of panic. "I thought you wanted to observe her until dinnertime?" It was only three in the afternoon. He'd been hoping to stick around until five or six.

"Relax, Dad. Mom and baby are doing great. You'll meet your new son or daughter soon enough." Dr. Regner glanced at her watch. "I have to check on another patient, but I would like to see Olivia back in the clinic next week."

"Understood." Ryker hoped the danger would be over by then. "We can do that."

Olivia raised a brow, no doubt wondering why he'd included himself, but didn't argue. "Thanks, Dr. Regner. I appreciate everything you've done for me."

"Of course. Now don't hesitate to call if the contractions return. I have a feeling this baby isn't going to stay put until your actual due date."

"And you're sure it's okay for her to be discharged?" Ryker couldn't help attempting one more time to convince the doctor to change her mind.

"I'm sure. The nurse will be in shortly with your discharge paperwork." Dr. Regner turned toward the door. "Don't forget, one week."

"I won't forget." Olivia's smile didn't quite reach her eyes and he knew she didn't want to go.

He didn't, either.

When they were alone, Olivia said, "I guess this is it."

"It's going to be okay." He kept his tone confident as he pulled out his phone to call Marc. They needed a safe house ASAP. Then he filled Tony Seavers in on the plan.

He wasn't going to allow any of Kevin Blake and Harper Moore's men to touch her again.

Olivia knew she needed to stay calm and strong for the baby's sake. All along, she'd understood stress wasn't good for her, and this latest bout of labor only reinforced her belief.

Ryker was on the phone again, talking to Marc Callahan about securing a place for them to go. She stopped listening, deciding to talk to her baby instead.

"We're going to be fine, little lady," she crooned. "I want you to stay inside where you can grow big and strong for just a little longer, okay?"

The baby kicked, making her smile. She looked forward to the day she would hold her daughter in her arms and tried not to think about how it was unlikely she'd have more children in the future.

Her gaze strayed to Ryker, wondering what he'd do once the danger was over. Would he find another single mother to rescue? How many were out there, needing his skills? She had no idea, but felt certain if there was someone in danger, Ryker would be all over it.

He'd never hesitate to save others because he hadn't been there to rescue his girlfriend and her daughter. It was disconcerting to realize she was a stand-in for the woman he'd really loved.

"Yeah, we'll take it. Thanks, Marc." Ryker turned toward her. "Good news. One of the FBI agents in Madison is arranging for a hotel suite. It's not far, roughly ten minutes from here."

"I'm glad." She couldn't deny feeling relieved. "Does that mean Aaron can join us?"

Ryker hesitated. "Maybe. Let's get you settled there first, then we can discuss our options with Mike."

She nodded. The nurse entered the room with her usual cheery smile. "I'm going to discontinue the monitor on your belly and take your IV out, okay?"

Liv wanted to protest about the monitor. She'd enjoyed seeing the reassuring beat of her baby's heart on the screen.

The IV came out first, then the monitor. Free of cables and IV tubing, she swung her feet around to sit up at the side of the bed.

"Do you need help getting dressed?" The nurse glanced at her, then Ryker.

Ryker made a coughing-choking sound. "I need to talk to Tony for a moment. Why don't you help Olivia get dressed?"

The nurse looked surprised when Ryker slipped out the door, but didn't seem to mind helping Olivia off the bed and into her own clothes. Oddly enough, Olivia felt stronger now than she had before she'd been put in the hospital bed. Clearly, she needed to stay hydrated, even if that meant frequent trips to the bathroom.

"Sit down. I'll be back with a wheelchair." The nurse left and Olivia quickly used the restroom while Ryker was outside. He came back with the nurse.

"Duncan is going to pick us up in the corner of the parking structure not far from the doorway," he informed her as she took a seat in the wheelchair. "We'll need to give him about five minutes to get here."

"Five minutes?" The nurse frowned and looked at her watch. "I'll take you down to the lobby. You can wait for your ride there."

"No need. I can take care of pushing Olivia in the wheelchair." Ryker didn't seem to like the idea of going to the lobby. "Just give her the discharge paperwork."

"If you're sure." The nurse hesitated, then shrugged. "Okay, that should be fine. Here are your discharge instructions, Olivia. Dr. Regner wants to see you in her clinic next week, so we made an appointment for you on Wednesday at one o'clock in the afternoon."

"Wednesday at one is fine." At least, she hoped this nightmare would be over by then. She took the proffered paperwork with a smile. "And I know I'm to call if the contractions start up again."

"Exactly."

"Thanks again." Liv meant it. She was grateful for the labor-and-delivery team's expertise and knew she wanted to return to this hospital when it was time to have her baby.

"You're welcome." The nurse hurried out of the room, obviously in a rush to check on her other patients. Olivia didn't blame her.

She glanced at Ryker. "Is Agent Seavers going with us?"

"I think so. If not, he'll hand us over to Agent Barnes. He's the one who arranged the hotel."

She smiled. "I'm glad Blake-Moore has no idea I'm here."

A frown creased his brow. "I hope not, but we're taking added precautions just in case."

The minutes dragged by slowly as they waited

for Duncan's call. When it finally came, the shrill ringtone startled her.

She took a deep breath, reminding herself to stay calm. No Stress was her new mantra.

"Got it. See you soon." Ryker put his phone away and came to stand behind her wheelchair. "Ready?"

"Yes." Ignoring the pang she felt in leaving the safety of the hospital room, Liv kept her gaze focused straight ahead. As they passed Tony in the hall, he nodded and fell in step behind them.

Ryker pushed her into the elevator, hitting the button labeled Lobby.

"I thought we were avoiding the lobby?"

"Originally, but there's a connection from the lobby level to the parking garage. That's where Duncan is meeting us."

Her entry into the hospital through the emergency department was nothing but a blur so she didn't question his knowledge.

They made it through the lobby and into the parking garage within the promised five minutes. When Agent Seavers's phone rang, he looked at his screen and grimaced. "My boss, likely mad at the way I let Seth get to Olivia. Give me a minute, okay?" Seavers brought the phone to his ear, turning away to speak in private.

"I think I see Duncan." She gestured to the black SUV. "Stop, Ryker. I'll walk from here."

Ryker set the brakes on the wheelchair, putting his hand beneath her elbow to help her to her feet.

She'd only made it a few steps when a blur of movement caught the corner of her eye. She turned her gaze in time to see a man she recognized as one of the bosses Tim had introduced her to at the Fourth of July party. He stepped out from behind a concrete pillar, holding a gun trained on them.

"Don't move." His tone was terse.

She froze, her hands splayed protectively over her belly.

"What do you want, Moore? Or is it Blake?" Ryker's question was mild, as if he wasn't the least bit worried about the armed man standing there.

"Moore. And you know what I want." He waved the gun. "Give me the account numbers now!"

"B-but, I don't have them." Olivia couldn't seem to drag her gaze from the muzzle of his gun. If he pulled the trigger, she and her baby would die. Thankfully, Aaron was safe, but she didn't want her son to become an orphan.

"I have them," Ryker said. "But I want Olivia safe first."

"No deal." Moore lifted the gun a bit higher.

Ryker began to recite the numbers by memory, then stopped abruptly, narrowing his gaze on Harper Moore. "If you want the entire account number, you'll let me send Olivia off with my friend. You don't need her when you have me."

"No!" She didn't want to leave Ryker behind. She couldn't bear the thought of losing him.

She loved him. More than she thought possible.

And she knew, deep in her bones, that once Harper Moore had what he wanted, he'd kill Ryker.

SEVENTEEN

More than anything, Ryker wanted to protect Olivia. To keep her safe from harm. Yet here they were, being held at gunpoint by a cold-blooded killer. Ryker swallowed a lump of guilt, knowing he should have anticipated Blake-Moore would find them at the hospital.

So much for Seth Willis's claim of not being involved with the mercenary group. Obviously, Willis must have been acting on orders from Harper Moore himself. Did that mean Kevin Blake knew about the money, too? Or had the partner of the firm been left in the dark? There was no way to know for certain.

"You can't possibly remember all the bank-account numbers," Moore said with a sneer. "You're rattling off garbage. Send Olivia to me, and I'll let you and your friend live."

No way was he doing that. Moore would kill her and the baby without a second thought. He actually did know all the numbers. He'd memorized them just in case, but wasn't sure how to convince Moore. He decided to try a different path. If he stalled long enough, maybe Duncan could get a shot at him. At the moment, he and Olivia were in Duncan's way, and Ryker knew Duncan wouldn't risk hitting Olivia. Or maybe Tony Seavers from the FBI would arrive to help. That phone call from his boss was rotten timing.

At this point, he'd welcome anyone, even someone from the hospital security team.

"Tell me, Harper, when did you learn Tim and Colin were skimming money from you and Kevin? I'm sure that made you furious."

The question caught Moore off guard, but he didn't hesitate to answer. "Seth told me what he knew. I offered to give him a finder's fee if he brought me the bank-account information, but he got himself arrested instead." The barrel of Moore's gun never wavered. "Enough talking. We need to move. I want Olivia with me now!"

Ryker met Olivia's frightened gaze and knew he needed to do something to get her out of this mess. He swept his gaze over the area in an attempt to formulate a plan. The gun he normally kept on him at all times was in the glove box, because the hospital had a no weapon rule. There had to be something he could do.

But there was absolutely nothing to use as a

weapon. The wheelchair and garbage can were both too far away to be of any use.

He prayed for strength and wisdom, hoping God had a plan for them.

"Oh!" Olivia let out a loud groan, doubling over in pain. "Help me! The labor pains are back."

What? Now? Ryker felt the blood draining from his face. Her labor must have restarted because of the stress.

"Hurry!" Moore's tone was sharp. "I want the information before she drops that kid."

"Don't be stupid." Ryker lifted his hands up in a gesture of surrender. "You don't need her when you can have me."

Olivia slowly blinked her eyes at him, and it took only a second for him to realize she was pretending. He decided to play along. "Olivia? How bad are they?"

"Bad." Her voice was low and guttural. "If I don't get inside, I'll have this baby right here in the parking garage!"

"Take me." Ryker drilled Harper Moore with his gaze. "She'll be useless to you while she's in labor. And I promise I have the bank-account numbers memorized. Don't you see? She's a liability to you. She needs a doctor!"

"Fine. I'll take you. Stuff her into the SUV."

Moore gestured with the gun. "One false move and I'll shoot."

Ryker doubted the guy would shoot in a public place, even if they were in a rather isolated corner of the parking garage. But Ryker was more than willing to comply with his demand. Olivia was still bent over, pretending to be in pain, so he moved close. "Lean on me. I'll get you into the SUV, okay? Duncan will get you out of here."

"But what about the doctor?" Olivia sounded fearful and he hoped he hadn't misunderstood her exaggerated blink. That she really wasn't in labor.

"You'll be fine." He knew that his gun was in the glove box of the SUV. All he needed was the opportunity to grab it.

As it turned out, Duncan already had the glove box open. As if reading his mind, Olivia lurched forward toward the passenger seat, staying low to give Ryker access to the gun.

Ryker knew Duncan was armed, but seated as he was behind the wheel, his buddy couldn't shoot without possibly hitting him or Olivia, considering Harper Moore was located behind them. Ryker knew he'd have to be the one to take the shot.

He pushed Olivia down toward the floor and reached for the weapon.

Several things happened at once. A loud, authoritative voice shouted, "Hey, what's going on?" At the same time, Ryker spun around to shoot at Moore. Moore must have been momentarily distracted by the man approaching the scene, because he didn't even get a shot off.

Blood spurted from Moore's chest. He sagged against the concrete pillar, then slowly slid to the ground, a look of stunned surprise on his features.

Duncan hit the horn, the blare echoing loudly off the concrete surrounding them. The approaching security guard and other people arrived on the scene from various directions, including Tony Seavers from the FBI, looking guilty for not staying with them.

Ryker rushed over to check on Harper Moore, who was pale and bleeding, but still alive. "Where is Kevin Blake?"

Moore struggled to speak. "Dea…"

Dead? "Come on, tell me where Kevin Blake is." Ryker pressed his hand against the wound, hoping to stem the bleeding. "We need an ambulance now!"

"I'll call," the security guard offered.

"You're not going to die, Harper, but you will spend the rest of your life in jail." Ryker leaned his weight on the wound, peering down into Harper's eyes, willing the guy to respond. "Do you really want Kevin Blake to get away with all the cash?"

"He's dead…" Harper Moore's eyes drifted closed and his jaw went slack.

No! Feeling frantic, Ryker continued holding pressure on the gunshot wound. "Harper! Wake up!" He raised his head, looking at the various bystanders who were blatantly gawking. "I need a doctor here now! Hurry!"

"They're on the way." The security guard came over to kneel beside him. "What can I do?"

Ryker shook his head. "I don't want him to die. The FBI has been searching for this guy and his partner. He can't die!"

"Okay, I get it." The security guard rested a hand on Ryker's shoulder. "Are you a cop?"

"Not exactly." Ryker wondered if he'd be arrested for shooting the guy, despite the fact that he'd only done it to save Olivia's life. "I need you to secure the video for this parking garage. The Feds will want to review it."

The security guard's eyes widened as he nodded. "I can do that."

"Good." Where in the world was that medical team?

"Speaking of which, Marc Callahan is on his way." Tony Seavers gestured at the area around the SUV. "He'll work with the locals to clear the scene."

"Olivia?" Ryker craned his neck in an attempt to make eye contact with her. "Are you all right? You're not really in labor, are you?"

"I'm fine." She stood leaning against the SUV, with Duncan beside her. "Don't worry about me."

He nodded, but couldn't relax. Hearing the pounding of footsteps on the ground, he was grateful to see several men and women wearing scrubs rushing toward him. He didn't move, not until the medical team was close enough to take over.

"Gunshot wound to the chest." He moved out of the way. The team surrounded Harper Moore, the tall redheaded female obviously in charge.

"Get his chest wound packed with dressings. Get his vitals."

Ryker stared at his blood-stained hands with a sense of dismay. He didn't regret doing what was necessary to save Olivia's life, but wished he hadn't hit Moore in the chest. If the guy didn't make it, they'd be no closer to finding Kevin Blake.

"So much blood," Olivia whispered.

He grimaced, knowing she was right.

"Why don't you wash up?" She gently tugged

on his elbow. "You're covered in blood and the restrooms aren't far."

He didn't want to leave her alone, but he didn't want to get her covered in blood, either. He followed her back inside the hospital to the restrooms just off the main lobby. After scrubbing the blood from his hands, he returned to find her waiting for him. Ryker longed to pull her into his arms, but noticed Marc Callahan striding toward them.

"You okay?" Marc's keen gaze raked over him. "No injuries?"

"I'm fine. Olivia's the one who needs to see a doctor."

"No, I'm okay." Olivia turned toward Marc. "Moore wanted the bank-account information."

"He claims Seth Willis told him about the embezzlement scheme," Ryker added. "He didn't say one way or the other if Kevin Blake was involved. When I asked where Kevin was, he said *dead.*"

"I'll need to corroborate his claim that Blake is dead, although it doesn't make sense Moore would lie about that. Why would he want Blake to get all the cash?" Marc blew out a heavy sigh. "We're going to need your statement and Olivia's before you can leave."

"Duncan's, too." Ryker knew the drill. "I asked the security guard to secure the video.

Figured you and the local authorities will want to review it."

"We will." Marc held out his hand. Ryker solemnly shook it. "Nice work. Glad you were able to stop him."

"Thanks." Ryker noticed the medical team was bringing Harper Moore's gurney inside, in a flurry of activity. The beeping heart monitor was somewhat reassuring, but the grim expressions on the faces of the team members told him that Moore was only hanging on by a thread. He couldn't seem to tear his gaze away as they wheeled past him.

"It's not your fault." Olivia's soft voice drew him from his dark thoughts. "He made the decision to come after me with a gun in an effort to get his hands on the money."

"I know." He pulled her close and buried his face against her silky hair. "I'm so glad you're okay."

"We both are." The baby kicked, making him smile. "Actually, all three of us are. You saved us again, Ryker. I'm sorry you've had to face so much violence to do it." Her body shuddered as if the memory was horrifying to her.

And he couldn't blame her.

Emotion clogged his throat, and for a moment he couldn't speak. Violence. She'd witnessed him doing violent acts from the moment they'd met. All along he knew that once Olivia returned to her normal everyday life, there would be no place for him.

Now he realized that the opposite would be just as bad. Having him around would only make her remember the horrible things she'd witnessed. All the blood she'd seen spilled.

Now that Harper Moore was out of the picture, and Kevin Blake was likely dead, there was nothing more for him to do.

It was time to let Olivia and Aaron go. To give them the normal life they deserved.

She relished being held in Ryker's warm embrace, but it was over all too soon. He eased away, looking at Marc. "Let's get these statements out of the way as soon as possible. Olivia wants to see Aaron and deserves to get some rest."

"Olivia can speak for herself, thanks." She wasn't sure why Ryker's tone irked her. It seemed as if he was pulling away from her. "I'm *fine*."

Marc's lips twitched. "Okay, I'll talk to Olivia over here. Tony Seavers will take your statement."

Ryker gave a curt nod and moved away, without giving her a second glance. She frowned, wondering what was going on with him. She knew Ryker was likely feeling a bit of guilt over his role in taking down Harper Moore, but it wasn't as if there had been an alternative.

Marc Callahan led her to a seat in the corner of the lobby cordoned off from the rest of the public. Plenty of gawkers still hung around, but the hospital security guards were doing their best to send them on their way.

"Start at the beginning," Marc suggested.

As she told the story, Marc interrupted her several times, asking additional questions. The process took far longer than she would have expected, but finally he nodded, his expression full of satisfaction.

"Okay, thanks, Olivia. Would you like me to contact Mike so you can talk to Aaron?"

"Yes, please." When he handed her his phone, she lifted it to her ear. "Aaron? Is that you, sweetheart?"

"Mommy! When are you coming to get me?"

"Soon, baby. Very soon. Are you being a good boy for Mr. and Mrs. Callahan?"

"Yes. Mommy, Brodie's daddy wants to talk to you."

"Okay, but just know I'll see you soon, Aaron." There was a brief silence before she heard Mike's voice. "Hey, heard Ryker got Harper Moore."

"Yes. But there's still Kevin Blake."

"I heard Blake is probably dead," Mike said reassuringly. "If he and Moore both knew about the money, they'd have worked together to get to you."

"Gee, thanks. That's so not reassuring."

"Sorry, but it's the truth. Do you want me to bring Aaron to you? Just tell me when and where."

"Anxious to get rid of him, huh?" Her wry smile faded. "Actually, I'm not sure where I'm supposed to go. There was a hotel room, but I'm not sure if that's still on. Let me find Ryker and we'll call you back, okay?"

"Sure, no problem. And really, there's no rush. Aaron and Brodie are playing together just fine."

"Thanks, Mike. You and Shayla are lifesavers." She handed the phone back to Marc. "Your family has been wonderful to us."

Marc waved off her gratitude. "We owe Ryker and Duncan for the way they helped us in the past. No need to worry about it. Would you like to return home?"

"Home?" She thought about the house she'd once shared with Tim. The one she hadn't seen in six months, and thought she'd never see again. The idea of returning there wasn't very appealing, but what choice did she have? Staying in motels for the indefinite future wasn't exactly an option. "Sure, I guess."

Marc frowned at her lackluster tone. "We can go to the hotel instead. It's already been arranged."

"No, it's fine. I'm being silly." She forced a smile. "Although, I would like Ryker to come with me. At least for a day or two."

Marc lifted a brow. "I'll get him. He's likely finished with his statement by now."

"Thank you." The thought of having Ryker stay with her filled her with relief. Everyone involved in the case seemed convinced Kevin Blake was dead, but how could they know for sure? Granted, Mike had a point about the fact they would have been working together if they'd both known about the money.

Marc returned with Duncan, a sheepish expression on his face. "Um, looks like Ryker already left, but Duncan agreed to take you home."

Left? Why would Ryker have taken off without telling her?

Without so much as saying goodbye?

Her heart seemed to stop in her chest. Obviously, Ryker felt his job of protecting her was over. He hadn't really cared about her and Aaron, not the way he'd loved his girlfriend and her daughter.

"Olivia? Are you ready?"

She drew in a deep breath, trying not to let her despair show on her face. "Um, sure. But will you please call Mike to let him know? He offered to bring Aaron."

"Of course." Duncan took a few steps away, speaking quietly into the phone for a few minutes before turning back to her. "He'll meet us at your place."

She nodded and wearily pushed herself to her feet. She followed Duncan back out to the parking structure where he'd left their SUV. She was surprised it wasn't being held as evidence, but remembered Ryker saying something about the security video. Maybe that was all they needed.

She was happy to leave the hospital and to know she'd be seeing Aaron again soon.

But the hollow feeling in her chest wouldn't go away.

Ryker's leaving had put a gaping hole in her heart and she knew that her life would never be the same without him.

EIGHTEEN

Walking away from a woman had never been so difficult. Ryker's heart felt as if it were being ripped out of his chest. He already missed her.

But their time together was over.

She needed to move on, and he knew having him around would only be a horrible reminder of the danger she and Aaron had been in. The violence she'd witnessed. Seeing all that blood had made her shiver.

She'd get over him, even if he wouldn't get over her.

His role in life was to save others, the way he'd always wished someone had stepped up to help his girlfriend and her daughter. Now that his mission was accomplished, it was time to move on.

Olivia would be fine with Duncan and Tony, but by the time he'd called a rideshare for a pickup, he was already doubting his decision to leave.

Shouldn't he at least say goodbye? Let her know that if anything changed for her in the future, she could reach out to him? What if the violence didn't bother her the way he'd thought it did?

The rideshare driver pulled up in a fancy black BMW. He was staring through the passenger window at Ryker impatiently. "Well? Are you coming?"

"No." He turned and headed back through the parking structure to the hospital entrance. He frowned when he noticed Duncan's SUV was gone.

His heart squeezed and he quickened his pace. When he burst into the lobby, he raked his gaze over the area, looking for a familiar face.

"Marc!" He rushed toward the FBI agent. "Where's Olivia?"

"She left with Duncan and Tony." Marc frowned. "Tony said you left."

"I'm back." He couldn't believe he'd missed them. "Where are they headed? To another hotel?"

"No, she's going home." At Ryker's blank look, Marc added, "You know, her house. Where she once lived. Mike is bringing Aaron out to Madison to drop him off there."

The home she'd shared with Tim? Every cell in his body rejected that idea. "Why would you let her go there? Did you confirm Kevin Blake is dead the way Harper Moore claimed?"

"She can't very well stay in a hotel indefinitely. But to answer your question, we're still working on validating Blake is dead. But even if by some freak chance he's not, the mercenary group is done. If Harper Moore survives, he'll spend the rest of his life in jail."

It made sense, but Ryker still didn't like it. He turned and walked back outside, pulling up the rideshare app on his phone.

The same driver pulled up, eyeing him warily. This time, Ryker slid into the back seat of the Beamer, reciting Olivia's address.

He sat back against the leather seat, trying to think of what he'd say to her when he saw her again. He wanted to support her, without being a constant reminder of the danger she'd been in.

There was no doubt he wanted to be there when her baby was born. But again, he wasn't so sure she wanted him. She'd leaned on him at the hospital, but that was when she was anticipating a premature birth.

Her due date was less than six weeks away. Would they still be talking to each other? Or would they have already drifted apart?

He had no idea. But at the very least he could provide his contact information, before walking away.

He'd leave it up to her to make the next move.

* * *

Olivia felt ridiculously nervous when Duncan pulled up in front of her small house. Oddly, it looked different.

Or maybe she was the one who'd changed. In her head she knew the house was just a structure, but she couldn't help but shiver as she stepped out of the SUV.

"Wait here with Tony." Duncan glanced at the house. "I want to do a quick search of the place before you go inside. Just to be sure no rogue mercenaries are hanging around."

She nodded, secretly glad to postpone the inevitable for a while longer. The more she thought about it, she knew she'd end up going to a motel once Aaron arrived. Even if Blake was dead, she didn't feel comfortable here.

This house represented a chapter of her life that was over and done. Time to move on with the next phase. The sooner she could put the place on the market and unload it, the better.

Tony Seavers came up beside her and pressed something hard into her side. "You're going to walk away with me, understand?"

Huh? She belatedly realized he held the muzzle of a gun against her. "You? You're involved?"

"Let's go." Tony pressed the gun against her,

leaving her little choice but to take a step away from Duncan's SUV.

"Did Harper Moore or Kevin Blake put you up to this?" She wanted to keep him talking, hoping Duncan would return before they could get very far. She wasn't sure where Tony was taking her, not that it mattered much. In her condition, she couldn't make a run for it.

"Blake isn't dead, although we faked his demise to throw Moore off track. Kevin is meeting us soon." Tony walked her farther from the house, looking up and down the street. Everything made so much more sense now. The way he'd let Seth in to see her, the way he'd hung back, leaving them to go into the parking garage alone to meet up with Harper Moore.

Now this.

"It was you and Blake against Seth and Harper Moore, wasn't it?" The fact that each owner had tried to outdo the other was so obvious now, she couldn't believe they hadn't considered the possibility sooner.

"Think you're smart, huh? But I have you now."

She swallowed hard, wishing Ryker was there with her. But he wasn't.

And if Tony Seavers and Kevin Blake had their way, she'd never see Ryker, or Aaron, again.

Tears pooled in her eyes and she tried to blink

them away. She had to be smart. There had to be something she could do to get away.

She glanced at the nearby houses, trying to remember the names of her neighbors. But she didn't see anyone, much less someone she actually recognized.

A black BMW pulled up beside them. Her heart momentarily stopped in her chest as she frantically searched for a way to escape.

The driver's-side window opened only an inch. "Get in."

"Will do." Tony must have been expecting a car sent by Kevin Blake to pick them up. He held her in place as the driver rolled the window back up and edged the vehicle ahead a couple of feet.

The door behind the driver was opened by someone inside. Tony pushed her in and she stumbled, catching herself by grabbing on to the edge of the door.

A quick glance inside revealed Ryker's familiar face. Her heart soared. He'd come for her! With a quick movement, he tugged her toward him.

"Go!" Ryker shouted to the driver.

The BMW lurched forward, the rear door swinging shut behind her.

"Hey!" Tony shouted after them.

"He has a gun!" She reached for Ryker. "Keep your head down."

"Gun?" the driver shouted. "You didn't say anything about a gun!" The wheel jerked beneath his hands. "What if he shoots at me?"

"Just keep going," Ryker barked. Then he turned toward her. "Are you okay? Did he hurt you?"

"F-fine." She stared at him. "How did you know?"

"I didn't at first, but as soon as I saw the two of you together, I figured it out. And convinced the Uber driver to play along." Ryker pulled out his phone. "I have to call Duncan."

"Tony is waiting for Kevin Blake to arrive. He's not dead after all."

Ryker let out a low whistle. "I'm glad I beat him."

"Me, too." She wanted to ask him why he'd left her in the first place, but he was quickly filling in Duncan on the latest turn of events.

Next he called Marc and brought him up to speed. "Tony Seavers is working with Blake. I need you to send a team to Olivia's house ASAP."

She couldn't hear what Marc said in response. Ryker slid his phone into his pocket, then leaned forward to tap the driver on the shoulder. "Take a left here, then another left."

"Hey, I'm not going back there," he protested. "That's crazy."

"Take two left turns, then drop us off." Ryker had no sooner said the words when the sharp report of gunfire could be heard behind them.

"Duncan!" She covered her mouth with her hand, feeling sick, praying that Tony, or Kevin Blake, hadn't shot him.

"Hurry," Ryker urged the driver.

"Where's your gun?"

"Tony took it back at the hospital, said he needed it for evidence." Ryker's expression was grim. "It's protocol after a shooting, so I didn't think much about it."

"We can't go back there without any way to protect ourselves." Her voice rose with panic. "Tell the driver to take us away."

"I can't leave Duncan alone." Ryker met her gaze. "I still have a knife."

A knife? Against a gun?

The driver did as Ryker suggested, bringing the car to a screeching halt. Ryker threw a wad of cash at the guy, then helped her out and took her hand.

"This way." He gently tugged on her hand, cutting through several backyards in an effort to return to help Duncan. As they approached a line of trees, a man suddenly came barreling out toward them, a gun in his hand.

Kevin Blake! The moment she recognized him, Ryker let go of her hand and rushed toward him. Blake lifted his weapon, but didn't get a shot off before Ryker tackled him to the ground.

"Help! Someone help!" She yelled at the top of her lungs, hoping and praying someone would come to help Ryker. She held her breath as the two men struggled for the gun.

Ryker was younger and in better shape, but he'd also been going on very little sleep. She couldn't predict the outcome, but she could help him. Quickly she surveyed the area for a potential weapon—a downed branch, a discarded garden tool. Anything.

As she sent up a silent prayer, she saw Marc Callahan tear through the tree line, just as Ryker managed to get the upper hand on Kevin Blake.

Then it was over. Marc cuffed Blake's wrists as Ryker rose to his feet, immediately searching for her.

"Ryker." Her breath caught in a sob as she ran over to hug him. He caught her close, pressing his mouth to her temple.

"Shh, it's okay. It's all over. You and Aaron are safe now."

"Duncan has Tony Seavers," Marc said with satisfaction. "Looks as if each owner found his own accomplice in an effort to outdo the other. Come on, Blake. Time for you to go for a little ride." Marc dragged him back toward her house, where his vehicle was parked at a sharp angle, no doubt abandoned in a hurry.

She leaned heavily against Ryker, trying to absorb the fact that this nightmare was truly over.

"You aren't in labor again, are you?" Ryker asked.

She shook her head, unable to bring herself to let him go. He didn't seem to mind, cradling her close and rubbing a hand down her back.

"Why did you leave me?" She lifted her head to search his gaze.

"I'm sorry. I shouldn't have left until we had evidence that Kevin Blake was actually dead." Ryker's expression was full of remorse. "I had no idea Tony Seavers was on the take, but looking back, it makes sense."

"I don't care about Kevin Blake or Tony Seavers, Harper Moore or Seth Willis." She wanted to shake some sense into him. "I care about you, Ryker. I was so hurt when you left without saying goodbye."

"I'm sorry," he repeated. "I should have let you know."

That wasn't what she wanted to hear. "Why, Ryker? Why did you leave me? Is it because I'm just another case to you? You wanted to save me and Aaron the way you couldn't save your girlfriend and her daughter? Is that all this was to you? A job?"

"No." Ryker leaned forward, resting his forehead against hers. "You and Aaron mean so much more to me than that."

"Then why?" She still didn't understand.

He sighed. "I was afraid that being with you would be a reminder of all the bad things that have happened over the past several days. I felt you shiver when you mentioned all the blood around Harper Moore. I thought you might want to move forward with a clean slate."

What she wanted was to move forward with him. But she wasn't reassured by his words. "First of all, you're wrong about what I want. What I need. And secondly, what do you want?"

"You." He said the word simply. "I want you, and Aaron and the baby." He placed his palm on her belly. "But I also know that your feelings for me are confused with gratitude."

"Don't be ridiculous." She scoffed at the idea, then realized she didn't know anything about Ryker's family or even where he lived.

Did it matter? She gazed into his eyes, remembering how she'd looked into his hazel eyes the night they met, when she'd wanted to make sure he wasn't like her late husband and brother. All she saw, then and now, was sweetness and compassion.

"Listen, I know things have been crazy since we met, but you need time to rest and relax." Ryker tucked a stray strand of hair behind her ear. "Take a break, Olivia. Spend time with your son. If you want to see me, all you have to do is to ask."

"I want to see you." The words popped out of her mouth before she could think. "I know I'm pregnant and not exactly in a position to say this, but I love you, Ryker. I fell in love with you the day you put your hand on my stomach and reveled in the movement of my baby. The way you've been so kind and caring to me and Aaron—well, I've never experienced that sort of tenderness before."

His expression was filled with doubt. "Any man would have done the same. Like Duncan. If he'd come to rescue you instead of me, you'd be with him."

She shook her head, irritated he'd mentioned that twice now. "No, Ryker, I wouldn't. I like Duncan and the Callahans I've met so far, but there's only you. I love you. And if you don't feel the same way, I understand. But don't confuse what I'm feeling with gratitude."

He looked down at her, but remained quiet. She had no idea what he was thinking, what he was feeling. Despair began to build inside her, till finally she saw a smile tug at the corner of his mouth. "Okay, I won't." He swept her close and kissed her, showing her without words how he felt.

Maybe it was too early for him to say the words. That was fine with her. She loved him enough to wait.

"Hey! You're trespassing on my property!" A cranky man shook his fist at them from the doorway of his house.

Ryker broke off the kiss and grinned at the guy. "Sorry, sir. We're leaving."

The man glared at them as Ryker took her hand and led her through the gap in the trees to the backyard of her house.

"Ryker?"

"Hmm?"

"Do you have a family?"

He hesitated, and her stomach clenched. "No, I was raised in foster care, until the army became my family. Now I have friends, who are like my family."

Her heart ached for him. "You deserve so much more."

"Oh, I don't know. I've done okay. My friends are awesome."

He was awesome. And he didn't seem to realize it. "You are an amazing man, Ryker. I love you."

He stopped and turned toward her, capturing both of her hands in his. "I love you, too, Olivia. So much it scares me. I know meeting you was part of God's plan for me and I hope you feel the same way."

"Oh, Ryker." She was touched by his reaffirmation of his faith. "I do. God sent me a wonderful man to protect me, and to care about me. I feel so blessed to have met you."

"Ditto." He cleared his throat. "I don't want to rush you, but I'd like to keep seeing you. And Aaron. I want to be there with you every day, until your baby is born, and every day afterward."

Her eyes misted. "I'd like that."

"Mommy!" Aaron's voice cut through the moment and she turned in time to see her son running toward her. Aaron clutched her around the legs, until Ryker scooped the boy into his arms. Then Ryker stepped close, putting his arm around her waist so that Aaron was cradled between them.

"I missed you." Aaron leaned over to wrap his arms around her neck.

"I missed you, too." She met Ryker's gaze over Aaron's shoulder and knew this was the first day of their new life together.

As a family.

EPILOGUE

Five weeks later

Ryker placed his arm around Olivia's shoulders as she continued to push. "Come on, sweetheart. You can do it."

"She's a stubborn one," Olivia said between gritted teeth.

"Hey, at least he almost waited until his due date." The baby's gender was an ongoing joke between them. Personally he didn't care one way or the other, but Olivia was convinced she was having a girl.

"You're doing great," Dr. Regner said encouragingly. "One more big push and your son or daughter will be born."

"That's what you said last time." Olivia sounded annoyed, but he understood that this was just part of the process.

"You can do it. Let me know when you're

ready." He waited for her to signal another contraction was coming.

"Now!" Olivia let out a groan as she pushed. Ryker did his best to support her although how in the world any woman survived childbirth was beyond him. He was sweating as much if not more than Olivia.

"There she is!" The baby immediately started to wail. "A beautiful baby girl!" Dr. Regner wrapped the baby in a cloth and brought her over to Olivia.

"I was right." Olivia looked down with awe at the baby cradled against her chest. "A girl. We have a girl!"

"She's beautiful, and so are you." Ryker blinked against the threat of tears. "You did it, Olivia. Aaron has a baby sister."

"He'll be disappointed," she said with a wry laugh.

"Nah, he'll get over it." Ryker kissed her, then put his hand against the baby's head. "I love you so much, Olivia."

"I love you, too." She looked up at him. "I'd like to call her Julia, in honor of your foster mother."

His eyes burned with emotion. "I'd like that."

For a long moment he gazed down at Olivia and their daughter. "Olivia, will you please marry me?"

It wasn't the first time he'd asked her. Technically it was the third, not that he was counting. Okay, yes he was. She'd always told him she loved him, but had wanted to wait until after the baby was born to commit to marriage.

Granted, she probably hadn't meant the exact moment the baby was born, but hey, why wait?

She looked up at him and smiled. "Yes, Ryker. I'd be honored to marry you."

Her agreement filled him with joy. "I love you." He kissed her again, knowing he finally had a family of his own, one he'd treasure every single day.

For the rest of their lives.

* * * * *

If you enjoyed this book, don't miss these other stories from Laura Scott:

Shielding His Christmas Witness
The Only Witness
Christmas Amnesia
Shattered Lullaby
Primary Suspect
Protecting His Secret Son
Soldier's Christmas Secrets

Available now from Love Inspired Suspense!

Find more great reads at
www.LoveInspired.com

Dear Reader,

I hope you enjoyed Ryker and Olivia's story. I just knew as I finished Hawk's book that Ryker and Olivia deserved to have their own happily-ever-after. And please know, that I haven't forgotten about Duncan. I'm hard at work plotting his story, too.

Thank you so much for the kind messages you've sent through my website or through social media. I'm blessed to have a truly amazing group of readers!

If you enjoyed this book, I would very much appreciate if you might take a moment to leave a review. These are very important to authors and I'm grateful for each one.

I love hearing from my readers and can be reached through my website at www.laurascott-books.com or through Facebook at Laura Scott Author or via Twitter @laurascottbooks. Anyone who signs up for my newsletter receives a copy of an exclusive free novella that is not for sale on any venue.

Yours in faith,
Laura Scott

Get 4 FREE REWARDS!

We'll send you 2 FREE Books plus 2 FREE Mystery Gifts.

Love Inspired books feature uplifting stories where faith helps guide you through life's challenges and discover the promise of a new beginning.

FREE
Value Over
$20

YES! Please send me 2 FREE Love Inspired Romance novels and my 2 FREE mystery gifts (gifts are worth about $10 retail). After receiving them, if I don't wish to receive any more books, I can return the shipping statement marked "cancel." If I don't cancel, I will receive 6 brand-new novels every month and be billed just $5.24 each for the regular-print edition or $5.99 each for the larger-print edition in the U.S., or $5.74 each for the regular-print edition or $6.24 each for the larger-print edition in Canada. That's a savings of at least 13% off the cover price. It's quite a bargain! Shipping and handling is just 50¢ per book in the U.S. and $1.25 per book in Canada.* I understand that accepting the 2 free books and gifts places me under no obligation to buy anything. I can always return a shipment and cancel at any time. The free books and gifts are mine to keep no matter what I decide.

Choose one: ☐ **Love Inspired Romance Regular-Print**
(105/305 IDN GNWC)

☐ **Love Inspired Romance Larger-Print**
(122/322 IDN GNWC)

Name (please print)

Address   Apt. #

City   State/Province   Zip/Postal Code

Email: Please check this box ☐ if you would like to receive newsletters and promotional emails from Harlequin Enterprises ULC and its affiliates. You can unsubscribe anytime.

Mail to the **Reader Service**:
IN U.S.A.: P.O. Box 1341, Buffalo, NY 14240-8531
IN CANADA: P.O. Box 603, Fort Erie, Ontario L2A 5X3

Want to try 2 free books from another series? Call 1-800-873-8635 or visit www.ReaderService.com.